Shaun Meeks lives in Toronto, Ontario with his partner, Mina LaFleur, where they own and operate their own corset company L'Atelier de LaFleur. Shaun is a member of the HWA and has published more than 50 short stories. His most recent work has appeared in *Midian Unmade: Tales of Clive Barker's Nightbreed, Dark Moon Digest, Shrieks and Shivers from The Horror Zine, Zippered Flesh 2, Of Devils & Deviants* and *Fresh Fear*. His short stories have been collected in *At the Gates of Madness, Brother's Ilk* and *Dark Reaches*. His debut novel, *Shutdown* was released in 2014, as was his novelette *Down on the Farm*. To find out more or to contact Shaun, visit www.shaunmeeks.com.

T0118847

Book 1:
Dillon the Monster Dick series

THE GATE
AT LAKE DRIVE

by
Shaun Meeks

Featuring a bonus short story,
The Undergarment Eater.

This is a work of fiction. The events and characters portrayed herein are imaginary and are not intended to refer to specific places, events or living persons. The opinions expressed in this manuscript are solely the opinions of the author and do not necessarily represent the opinions of the publisher.

The Gate at Lake Drive
All Rights Reserved
ISBN-13: 978-1-925148-77-0
Copyright ©2015 Shaun Meeks
V1.1 US

The Undergarment Eater
All Rights Reserved
Copyright ©2015 Shaun Meeks
First published in Dark Moon Books' *Dark Eclipse Issue 29* November 28, 2013, edited by Lori Michelle. Original publication was in third person point of view, but it has been adapted especially to first person point of view for publication with this novel.

This book may not be reproduced, transmitted, or stored in whole or in part by any means, including graphic, electronic, or mechanical without the express written consent of the publisher except in the case of brief quotations embodied in critical articles and reviews.

Printed in Palatino Linotype, Arno Pro

Melbourne, Australia
IFWG Publishing International
ifwgpublishing.com

This book is for my brother, James. You introduced me to so much weird shit in my life; I hope I can return the favour one day.

And as always for Mina. There's a lot of you in this story, and I only mean that in the best way possible. You inspire so much and I am truly grateful for it.

THURSDAY

One thing I love is puzzles, but that doesn't mean I like them in every part of my life. Sure, I like to sit on the toilet and solve a Sudoku puzzle, or depending on what I ate the night before, maybe three or four. That doesn't mean I want to do a job where I have to solve some Sherlock Holmes-esque crap, or take Advil from thinking too much. I prefer to work smart, not hard. You do some research, go in with a plan and take care of business. I'm not one of those people that always need a daily challenge. I much prefer going into a job knowing what I am about to face and then getting in and out. Preferably in one piece.

Easy as pie.

But when I walked into this place less than twenty minutes ago, I knew right away there wasn't going to be anything easy with this job. I had screwed up. I thought I knew what I was getting into, that I had a good idea of what I was going up against. I was obviously wrong.

The place smells. It's like a cross between burnt hair and a dirty diaper. To you that might not mean so much, but for me, it means that I messed up. The man who hired me to come to his place of business told me he'd seen a creature in his warehouse, something that was big and malformed. He said it only seemed to come out late at night, mainly when the place was empty. He had seen the thing lurking in the shadows and eating buckets of paint like they were yogurt.

Now to most people, that would seem weird, I'm sure. It's not every day that you see a monster, let alone one eating paint with the gusto of a fat kid at an ice cream buffet, but for me, it was business as usual.

I listened to him and figured that what he was talking about was a Pharryn, a creature from the Gastt realm. I had heard about their strange taste for latex products, if and when they found their way over to Earth, so it made sense. I checked my supplies and was happy to see that I had just what I needed to deal with it and send it back to where it had come from.

Or so I had thought.

As it turns out, what's here in the warehouse is not a Pharryn at all. I haven't seen it yet, but I have caught a whiff of the horrific smell in here with me and know it all too well. Very few of the demons or monsters that find their way to Earth manage to bring their odour along with them. After all, what comes over is not really the physical form of the creature. In easy terms, what crosses over; it is just their essence, or their soul. But a Gadden smells so terrible normally, that even the misty, ghost-like form of them smells like utter shit.

I open my bag and give it a quick scan and hope that I have an item in my kit to deal with it. I brought tools and weapons to deal with a Pharryn after all, so I may be in trouble. Luckily, I also brought my dagger. It has been carved, blessed and branded with so many curses and spells that it is good enough to deal with almost anything. The only problem is my dagger isn't huge and I will have to get in close to use it. Most of the things I deal with are sad and pathetic really, some of the weaker creatures out there, and Gaddens are some of the easiest to deal with. I have only dealt with one before and by the end of it, I had been covered in a strange milky vomit and needed sixteen stitches. Not the best result I've ever had.

I pull the knife from the bag and scan the room. I'm so ready to hunt.

There are open paint cans everywhere I look and I see a steady trail that leads to the back of the well-stocked warehouse. My guess is that the creature eats its fill, and then goes back into hiding as soon as it's done. Although Gaddens are known to be a handful, they will hide when they are on Earth. Even the most violent and evil of the creatures I deal with will hide whenever they can. They all know they don't belong here, that there are rules and laws that forbid them from coming here. So as much as they want to be here and free from wherever they originated from, they want to keep their presence as secret for as long as they can. It's the fear of being sent back, of having to face the life they ran from and the punishment they will endure that makes them want to hide. And there's also me to deal with.

I'm not trying to toot my own horn here or anything, but the things that come here illegally, they all know about me. If they don't know me by name, they are aware of the others sent here to guard this world and send them packing should they break the rules. That's part of the reason they keep a lower profile. It's a good thing that most of them can't stay in the dark for too long. Most come out of hiding because something they want is here, or because they want to see the world they have been denied. I think a lot of them come here because they think there is something amazing on this world, hence the reason they are denied it. Others are running away from bigger problems and think this is safer than any other realm.

Whatever the reason, it doesn't matter. I have a job to do. And whether they come out to see this place or to find things they want; either way, it's a good thing for me. Makes hunting them so much easier.

I walk over to a sealed tin of paint and quickly open it. I use the tip of the knife to pop the lid, and step away from it, hoping the odour of it might draw out my shy Gadden. I find a hiding spot close by, let the shadows take me in and then I wait. I hope that it is dumb enough, or hungry enough to come out and get what I left for it.

I wait ten minutes before I see it. The creature slides out from under a shelving unit holding tools and boxes and I try and figure out what it is made of. When a creature crosses over to Earth, they leave their bodies in the world they are from and arrive here in a misty, ghost-like form. They have to use objects to re-form into something that has a semblance of their true shape. Usually what they end up using is trash, some discarded, inanimate object, but from time to time I have seen stranger things. Once I saw one inhabit a snake that had died days before. The weirdest one to date has to be the demon that found a home in a kid's mullet. That takes the cake. Usually, they have to use something dead, something that lacks a soul of any kind, but from time to time, there are ones that find a loophole in the way it works. Nothing is set in stone, and there are a lot of things in this and the other universes that just aren't predicable.

This time, the creature; the Gadden, must have found a bin of old rags and pop cans, because that is what its body looks to be made up of. There might be other pieces there, but that is the predominant make-up of the creature's new body.

The Gadden slinks slowly towards the open paint can and looks around, no doubt expecting a trap. I'm not sure how long it has been here in the warehouse, but I'm pretty sure this is the first time it has found dinner waiting. I've laid out something like a mousetrap for it, which should be obvious to anything with half a brain. And yet, it can't leave it alone. Like insects to a light. Sometimes, my job is easier than I think it's going to be.

Once the creature gets to the paint, it lifts the tin and begins to guzzle it as though it's a cold beer on a hot summer night. I hear it grunting, groaning and for a second I wonder how the Gadden is enjoying the paint. Does it have taste buds? Can it taste it at all, or is there some other source of pleasure it gets from it? I would love to know, but there is no point in trying to ask the thing questions, because as soon as I show myself, it's going to put up a fight. Once I step out of these shadows, dagger in hand, the Gadden is going to know the gig is up and it'll be one of those fight or flight situations.

I need to be quick and avoid any chance of flight.

While the Gadden is still lost in the pleasure of paint, I move around behind it, careful to be as quiet as I can. Then, before it can finish drinking or react, I take the dagger and jab it into the thing's leg. The blade screeches as it tears through a pop can, orange soda I think, and the warehouse is filled with the echoes of the damn thing's scream. The paint can drops, spraying the floor with eggshell semi-gloss and I pull the dagger free. As the blade cries out against the metal, paint gushes out of the wound as well as a light blue mist. I back up, hoping that it's enough to get the job done. I know that the idea of stabbing someone in the leg seems weak, as though there is no way anything would die from it, but the dagger is full of all sorts of magic and curses. It doesn't normally take much to dispatch some demon or monster from here with the smallest cut.

It's not working though.

That's not good.

The Gadden spins around, blue light glowing from the spots that I'm guessing are its eyes, and it pukes paint down the front of its makeshift body. Now that I'm beside it and it stands full erect I see that the Gadden is about seven and a half feet tall and I am worried about what comes next. The dagger either hurt it mortally, or I just pissed off an angry monster.

"YOU!" It cries out and takes a shaky step forward as I back away. "Dillon!"

"You know you're not supposed to be here. Time for you to go." I say and hold the knife out in front of me, hoping it's enough to hold the thing off.

"You're a fucking dick, you know that? Who did I hurt?" When it tries to take a second step towards me, the Gadden stumbles and falls to its knees. I hear more cans being crushed as it does. "I just wanted to be here, have some paint and get away from my world. It sucks there."

"Too bad. You know the rules. Nothing from outside the Earth realm is allowed here. You're not above those rules, so you know what I have to do now."

"Says who? Who made these stupid rules? Why can you be here and I can't? It's not fair!"

"I'm not going to argue with you. You know the way it

works, so deal with it. Earth is not a place you're allowed to go. You have no right to be here. Time to send you home."

"DON'T TOUCH ME!" it screams and tries to get up. I'm sure it wants to charge at me and no doubt use its substantial size advantage to do me in, so I back up a bit to see what it's going to do. I see it's having a hard time getting up and I know I have to take a chance here. I run in, thinking that it's now or never. I'm too hasty.

The creature reaches out and grabs me; its hand shifting so that it's like an octopus tentacle, wrapping around me and squeezing. I fight against it, use all my strength against the crush of its grip, but I struggle to breathe. Every breath I take in, the constriction gets tighter and tighter, making my intake shorter and more painful. I keep up the fight though, not wanting to give up and I hear the stupid thing laughing at me.

"Stupid fuck!" the Gadden cackles and crushes me even harder. "Now I'm going to do to you what you've done to so many. What happens when you die here?"

I try and say something witty, something to piss it off, but I have little to no air left in my lungs. I'm seeing dots in front of my eyes and I'm sure if I don't do something soon I'm going to black out, and then die. I'd rather that not happen. Death and I don't get along too well.

I use the last bit of strength in me to raise the dagger, and I swipe it across its face. The blade cuts through aluminum and the rags and it sprays my face in white paint. I feel the grip loosen right away. I gasp for air as my lungs burn and drop to the warehouse floor. I watch as the screaming Gadden falls backwards and hits the ground. It cries out in the gibberish of its own language. White paint pools under the body and I see more blue mist rising up from the wound.

Almost done.

I walk over to it, some of the rags and cans already falling away as his life force is no longer fully here, and unable to hold the false form it once had. It reaches a hand towards me, but I pay it no mind.

"You almost had me, big boy. Almost. But you know you will never get the upper hand. You have no right to be here, so it's bye for now. Let's not do this again, okay?"

And with that, I bury the blade into the chest of the Gadden and swipe downwards, ripping it in two. There is a geyser of blue light from its chest and then whatever held it together is gone and all that lies on the warehouse floor is the garbage it once called a body. I look down at myself, seeing what a mess I am and then the pain in my chest from being crushed returns as the adrenaline wears off.

I need a beer.

And some sleep.

I pull out my cellphone and text the owner to let him know the job is done and where he can send my payment.

FRIDAY

It's close to nine in the morning when my phone rings.

To say I'm not a morning person is like saying fish don't like to suntan. I despise the morning. I don't know why. It could be the happy chirping birds, or the kids rushing off to school; maybe the gridlocked roads or the overly-packed buses. Or it could be that I spend so much of my time running around at night that the early daytime make me feel like I'm an old school vampire. I may be able to move during the sun up, but I'm weaker than I would be at night. The only time I ever see my clock before noon is when someone wants something from me. Reluctantly, I reach over to my cellphone and look at the display.

Private number.

It would be.

The only people that call private number on this phone are people that have seen my website, my card or my TV ad that comes on the same time infomercials spam the airwaves. It means it's a work-related call. Part of me just wants to put the phone down, switch it to silent and fall back into the dream I was having.

Although I don't want to answer it, I do have a job and getting calls, even this early in the morning is part of it.

"Hello, this is Dillon the Monster Dick, how can I help you?"

Should I explain that?

I don't know if you're ever up late, watching TV while chugging down pop and eating junk food because you feel fat and somehow think it's a good idea to fight the lard with lard. Or you're feeling sad over money, your job, or someone that doesn't love you when you need it so you do what so many of us do to numb the pain; take a prescription of sugar, oil and bad television. At those moments, in the land of late-night television debauchery, is when you will see my ad pop up on the screen.

Some people, mainly Godfrey, always rag on me about the choice of my website and tag line. He thinks it makes no sense to call myself that and to have a website called *monster-dick.com*, but there is a method behind my madness. Whether it's demons, spirits, sprites or average monsters I am hunting down, people just think of these things as monsters. And calling myself a monster detective beats the hell out of monster exterminator or buster or whatever else you want to call it. A detective seems slightly more serious in my opinion.

As for the website, that's even easier and makes perfect sense to me. The idea starts with the fact that the internet is little more than a hub for porn. Sure, you might be watching videos, or going on some social networking site; hell, you may even be doing your taxes or homework. The fact is, that whatever you are doing that's not porn-related online, is usually just biding time until you either refill your reservoirs or you just need a break to avoid chafing.

So, knowing how people have a tendency towards those sites, I called my site Monster Dick, knowing that eventually people will run a search on it and then BOOM, there I am in front of you. Sure it wasn't what you were looking for, but I make it kitschy enough to keep people amused and they click it. I know they do because I check my analytics and I get over three thousand hits a day, usually new guests, and people stay on for somewhere close to ten minutes on average. Sure, you're not finding that huge monster wang you were looking for, but you find my site and laugh, thinking it's a big joke. Maybe you share it with your friends, which is also my hope. It's all good for me.

Why? Because one day, maybe tomorrow, you'll go down into your basement to get your stash of weed or Mad magazines and when you get down into that dark, stale smelling room, you'll see something. At first you'll think it's a trick of your eye. Maybe you'll try and blame it on that horror movie your friend made you watch. You'll laugh, say you're just being silly, but you'll see it again and again and know that something is down there.

Something not human.

That's when it comes back to you; that's when you remember my website and decide to call me up as the sun is trying to fuck my eyes from my skull and I'm waiting for you to talk.

"I think there may be a monster in my house."

And that's how most of these start, a statement that would sound crazy to most, but not to me. By now, I'm used to the idea that there will always be something in someone's house, or else why would I even be here?

It's a girl. She sounds young, but not too young to make me feel like a creep as I sit up and try to put on my professional voice.

"Has it made contact with you?"

"No."

"Is it violent or hiding?"

"Hiding. It runs whenever it sees me."

"What does it look like?"

"Well, um, that's the weird thing." It's always the weird thing. People usually think that when they see a monster that it

11

will be something big and ugly, a green lizard-like monsters or like a cartoon version of the devil, but they are never like that. The monsters and demons I deal with every day are not from here. They cross over and when they do, they leave their body behind and have to take up things to create a body here. Just like the Gadden at the warehouse. They come through a thin spot in the world, a place where their realm or world breeches this one and come here. Some of them need specific things in order to become solid. Once it was the soiled tissues of teenage boys—that was a very bizarre day. Whatever it is they use is not what an average human would expect from a monster. So, it's always weird.

"I've seen it all before. Just tell me as best you can what it looked like."

I hear her take a deep breath, no doubt doing her very best to build up the courage because she knows she must be going crazy. Everyone feels that way at first, when they see what they do, and then they call me. But since I have the website, the TV ads and even a mobile app, they hold onto hope that I will understand them and not judge too harshly.

Still, they never rush into it.

Better to let them talk in their own time.

While I wait for her to tell me all about it, I might as well go make some coffee. No way I'll be going back to bed, so why not? I'm listening to her describe something that only seems like a shadow, a shape she saw out of the corner of her eye. I'm making my coffee strong and sweet as she tells me that yesterday she went down to the basement again and saw it. This time, she was able to see what it really looked like because she brought a flashlight with her when she ventured down.

"Why were you going down there?"

"I know this sounds stupid, seeing as I told you how scared I was, but I was curious. I had to know what was there in my house."

Fair enough.

I sip my coffee; it's almost like mud, but it should do for waking me up.

"The thing moved all weird, like videos I've seen of newborn horses. So shaky and wobbly. I turned my flashlight on it, and it tried to run and hide behind some old boxes my mom had stored there when it was still her place. The thing fell and cried out as if it was scared of me. It was almost funny, but when I saw it fully, it quickly stopped being quite so funny."

It usually does. I've heard it before. People decide to go and comfort the things they see in the shadows, sure that it's only their eyes and mind playing a trick on them. And from time to time, I'm sure they are right, but when they call me, they've been wrong. They see something there, something their fragile minds have a hard time believing is true. But it's hard to deny it when you see some strange creature huddled in the shadows; a monster that can't be real. Most run then, and sooner or later they call me. They're in different stages of terror, sure that whatever it is that has invaded their house will come and get them, though for the most part, the trespasser is even more scared than they are.

"The thing looked like it was made up of shattered porcelain. This used to be my grandmother's house and she had a ton of those old Dalton figurines. When she passed, they were moved down to the basement, but I remember how they looked. The way those things have that same soft paint colouring; well this thing looked almost like washed out paint, but with a black hollow mouth and matching eyes. Totally creeped me the hell out."

"Did it say anything? Even something that didn't sound like any normal words to you?"

"It did! Wow, I wasn't even going to mention it because I didn't think it meant anything. When it cried it, it yelled 'tour lick' or something like it. Over and over again. Weird, huh?"

Not too weird. It sounds like the thing in her basement had said Tourik, which is a sort of prayer that a Thanilk would say; the equivalent of someone repeating 'Oh God' over and over. I hope that it is a Thanilk. They are not the toughest of the creatures I normally deal with, but I'm not going to tell her; she doesn't need to know that little tidbit. I get paid the same whether they're easy or hard to get rid of. Cash, credit or debt; no IOUs.

"Well, you're in luck, Ms…"

"Oh, sorry. I forgot to say. No Miss though. Just call me Rouge, everyone does."

"Okay, Rouge, well you're in luck. I am pretty sure that I know exactly what it is in your basement. When would be a good time to come over?"

"Now!" She says and laughs nervously.

"Well, now is not the best time for me. I would have to stop off somewhere to pick up a few items, but I can be there this afternoon, say around four or so?"

"That's cool, as long as it doesn't take too long. I have a show tonight and I can't miss it."

"No problem there. It would be better if you weren't there when I work anyway. No reason to put you in any kind of harm's way." This is a lie. The real reason I do these things alone,

14

especially with the monsters that tend to be chicken shits, is because it can get messy. There is usually a lot of screaming, sometimes violence, but there are usually things that happen which would make people question their sanity. No need to have them around to see it so I lie and say it's for their own good. And it makes me seem like I care and that I'm thinking only about them and their safety. "So what kind of show are you doing?"

"I'm a burlesque performer. Maybe you've heard of me: Rouge Hills?"

"Sorry, I don't get to go out too much."

"Too bad. You have no idea what you are missing."

I know she's right, but I don't say it. Instead we hammer out the details as I pour a second cup of muddy coffee and turn on the weather channel, hoping that it's not going to rain, but no such luck. Seventy percent chance of rain, and when I look out the window I see it's already raining. I shake my head. If it's already raining, doesn't that mean there is a one hundred percent chance of raining seeing as that's exactly what happening? Stupid weather channel.

Before I hang up, we come up with a price and agree to four o'clock. Now I try to figure out if I want to shower before I head to Godfrey's. He wouldn't care if I did or didn't; as long as he gets his money there isn't a whole lot else he cares about. If I were to say Godfrey was shady, that would be as oversimplified as saying the sun provides light. He is so much more than a shady character, but he is the only person I know that has what I need to do this job.

I figure I better have a shower. After all I am going to meet a burlesque performer, something I have never done before, so I might as well make a good impression. Not that I plan on hitting on her or anything like that, but you never know. I should also look up what a burlesque performer is, because in my head all I see is a fancy stripper, and I'm sure there's more to it than that.

I hate driving in the city. I think it's one of the most stressful things I do, and that is saying a lot since most days I hunt down monsters and demons. I feel trapped in my car, little more than a thousand pound coffin if I get in a bad accident, but what other choice do I have? Public transit? I would rather die in a terrible car crash than be subjected to that germ-infested hot box. I was on the subway once, and that was enough for me. A small, metal sardine can packed full of people than knew nothing of hygiene, manners or personal space. To say it was terrible is an understatement. I mean there is body odour and then there is the stuff of nightmares in the armpits and crotches of some people that use the buses and subways.

So I drive my coffin over to Godfrey's. It's a store, but looking at it from the outside it is a little hard to tell. There are no signs, nothing to let you know what might be inside. Most people pass it and think that it had gone out of business long ago. I guess you have to know Godfrey to know to go to him at all. Luckily I do.

The place looks about as inviting as a pedo van with a fat shirtless man driving it. The windows are dusty and barren, with a filthy white sheet hung behind to keep anyone from being able to see inside. There are bugs littering the windowsill and the door handle to the place has a strange green fungus has started to grow on the brass. There is no way someone who doesn't know what the store is about would ever want to want to enter and that's just the way Godfrey designed it. He has a very specific clientele and no doubt wants to keep it that way.

I walk into the dusty storefront that smells of wet metal and old dirt. The bell above the door jingles pathetically and within seconds Godfrey comes from the back room. He is smiling when he sees me there, showing off his teeth that seem slightly too big for his mouth, and he holds his hands out to me. His fingers are long and each one has a ring on them, with spells cast on them or charms buried deep into the metal.

"Dillon, my friend! So glad to see you here. When your business is good, mine is good. How can I help you today?" he says, with his thick Jamaican accent that isn't what it appears to be.

"I have a job this afternoon. Someone has what sounds like a Thanilk. What have you got for me?"

Godfrey makes a face as though he is considering the possibilities, as though he doesn't know exactly what to use. He does this every time. He's nothing if not a good salesman.

There are different weapons for different monsters and demons. Just like you wouldn't take a plunger to deal with a leaky roof, you wouldn't use certain weapons to fight certain creatures. Some only react to silver, others to symbols carved into wood or metal. Some have to be burnt with certain powders or liquids, while some will die by brandishing a mirror that was once housed in a cemetery. I know it sounds strange, but there are all kinds of rules that don't apply to humans. This world is very unlike the others that surround it. Other realms and worlds play by very different rules and most of the physics and science that people trust in here, mean nothing over there.

"I think I have the perfect thing for you!" Godfrey says and motions for me to follow him into the back. Once there I see things I know and others that I have never laid eyes on. Godfrey is always getting in new supplies and I've often wondered where he gets his supplies from, but he never tells me. Usually he just smiles and says that things have a way of finding him. "You did say a Thanilk, right?"

"Yeah. She said she heard the thing say something along the lines of Tourik, which means it has to be a Thanilk."

"That should be easy enough then. They aren't the most daring bunch, are they?" Godfrey laughs and starts walking beside the wall of shelves looking at different items and seems to consider each of them. I trust him in some ways, but I always get a strange vibe from him. He is a salesman after all, and I don't doubt that he would do anything to make a sale. In the past he has burned me, but there is nobody else in the city or the entire province that I can turn to. Godfrey is the only one I know that deals in these kinds of items. Tools made for killing, even if they don't look like it.

"So, does it matter if it might get messy?"

"Not really. From what the woman on the phone said the thing is made up of glass or porcelain, so I think it's going to get messy regardless."

"Then there is this."

Godfrey pulls what looks like a baseball bat off a shelf and walks over to me. The wood is dark, and as he comes close I see that there are markings, swirls and symbols and I know what they mean. Most weapons are etched with spells, curses or powerful words that control different things. If I were to use this bat on a human it would hurt them bad and if I hit them enough they would surely die. But if it has the proper inscriptions, it will dispatch a Thanilk with only one blow. Fast and easy: the way I like it.

Godfrey brings it over and looks happy, though he seems reluctant to let it go. Sometimes he wants the objects I use back; I don't know why, but he does. I can't always abide by his request though as sometimes these things get destroyed or I have to toss them so they can't be found. Once I had a strange gun, made of meat and bone from a creature not of this world, and though it was clearly not a conventional gun, it was not something I wanted to get spotted with. There were cops everywhere I turned that night so I had to toss it. It was a long weekend and the last thing I needed was to get pulled over by a cop to see if I was drunk and having it discovered. Not sure I would have been charged with any sort of crime, but I'd rather not be hassled or try to explain what it is I do. It's happened in the past and it never goes as smooth as I would like it to.

Godfrey was not too happy about it. He got so mad at me for throwing that one away that he threatened to stop selling to me. That didn't last long though. One threat about what would happen to him if he stopped and he knew that I was not bluffing on that point. He likes this planet too much I guess.

"I want this back, Dillon. I am serious. The wood used to make this was found off planet, in a cavern and brought to me specially. I want this for my collection when I finally retire."

19

"Like you'd ever retire. You love money and trade way too much for that."

"But dealing with you, someone that rarely pays me what I deserve; eventually I will get sick of it all."

"I promise I will do my best to return it." That's all I can do. You never know what's going to happen with a case. Sometimes I go in with the best intentions, a quick in and out, but it doesn't always work out. "Now you sure this will work?"

"Of course it will! Why would you even ask that?"

"Really Godfrey? Do we have to go through this every time? Have you ever given me the wrong thing, or lied in order to make a sale?"

"Oversights."

"Oversights my ass. You're as bad as a car salesman. Anything to close a deal, right?"

"Oh come now, Dillon. We've been friends for so long; why bring up the silly past?"

I nod. He knows that I am on to his ways. Still, who else am I going to go to? He has me by the short and curlies and he knows it. I list a few other items I need, some for Rouge's case, others just to restock my shelves. He gets me everything I need and we strike a deal that doesn't break my bank. It's more than I would like to spend, but I need everything he has so I pay and get ready to leave.

As I am about to go, he stops me and holds out something. I look down and it's a pair of gloves, like the ones I had ruined on a job recently. I had a job ridding a school of a creature that somehow crossed over to Earth with its own body. The thing was strong and nearly killed me, but I had used the gloves to hold him and ruined them when I took him apart in a pretty gruesome way. These gloves look almost like ones I lost before. They're leather and are woven with silver, gold and platinum, which are important when dealing with monsters and demons. They are spellbound with every charm known and make even the greatest foe unable to fight back. Along with my dagger, they work on almost anything I may come across and get close enough to grab.

"I know how much you like these. Try not to ruin these ones."

"Thanks." I tell him and tuck the gloves into my back pocket, and then leave the store to head over to Rouge's house.

I pull up to the curb and double check the address. When Rouge said she was a burlesque dancer, and then I did my research on them, for some reason I pictured a house straight out of an old fifties TV show. When I Googled burlesque, I saw people like Dita Von Teese in Marilyn Manson videos, pictures of Bettie Page, Tempest Storm, April March and others. Most the women looked very glamorous, not like strippers at the local peelers at all. Some of them were in places I assumed to be their home, so I had this specific picture of some 1950s bungalow with an old school car in the driveway. My idea was a house that would be like a Norman Rockwell painting mixed with some rockabilly kid's idea of what a vintage house should be.

The old Victorian beast stands three floors high catches me off guard until I remember she said that the place had been her grandmother's. Now I wonder what Rouge is going to look like.

Usually when I talk to people on the phone, I get a mental image of them. You can hear pitches and tones in their voice that reveal their personality and style. Seeing their house also helps. Getting out of my car and looking at the big house on the quiet side street, I wonder what the owner of the soft yet deep voice I spoke to on the phone is going to look like. My guess is that she will be one of those slightly awkward girls that looks like her heroes might include Buffy the Vampire Slayer and Velma from Scooby Doo.

I knock on the door, bag in hand. It's strange that I am thinking more about her than about the job at hand. I never do this.

The door opens and what stands before me is nothing close to what I expect. She is shorter than me, maybe five and a half feet with pale, almost alabaster skin and red hair done up into huge rolls that look amazing and difficult. Her lips are a deep red, glossy and slightly pouty and as I look down my eyes fall on the two bowling balls she seems to have stuck in her very form fitting dress. I know I must look like an idiot; no doubt my mouth is open as I stare at her, at a loss for words, no better than an adolescent boy. Come on hormones; calm down a bit.

"Would you like to take a picture, or at least lean your head over my flowers; they need a good watering."

"Uh…sorry." I stammer and try to make my mind get back into gear. I have a job to do. I hold my hand out to her, trying not to tremble. "I'm Dillon. You called me this morning."

"Really. Aren't you kind of young?"

"Not really. I look younger than I am, but trust me; I know what I'm doing."

"Is that why you stood there a second ago looking just like my little puppy when she watches me eat chips?"

"Sorry about that. I was…well…I know it wasn't very professional, but…" I'm stammering like an idiot. I wonder if I sound as dumb as I feel.

"I'm just kidding. If I didn't get a reaction like that out of people, I wouldn't be good at my job. Judging by your face, I picked the right outfit to show up at the venue tonight."

She smiles at me, and I silently I sigh a breath of relief. I will say this now; I am not good with attractive women, and Rouge is more than attractive. She is completely stunning. She's not one of those underfed models that look like they're walking down the runway so they can get another heroin fix, but she is by no means fat. She has a slim waist that is extenuated by her curvy hips and her very ample…

Damn, blood is rushing from my head; there is a demand in an area a little lower. I shift the bag a little so that it's in front of me and hope she doesn't notice the high school style movement. I feel stupid for my inability to act normal, but I do the best I can to disguise my discomfort.

"So, do you want to come in so I can tell you about what's going on?" she asks me while I stand still and silent.

"Um…actually, if you want to just grab whatever you are going to need for the night that would be better. We can talk in the front yard or driveway, where it shouldn't be able to hear us. Did you say you have a puppy?"

"Ah! Good thinking. And yes, I do, but no worries, my best friend is watching her until all this mess is over."

"Good."

She heads back into the house and once she is out of sight, I can relax. I realize that I have been standing there with my stomach sucked in the entire time. And it's not like I have a huge gut or something, yet I did it anyway. Strange. I make some quick adjustments to myself, tucking things up a bit to keep the bulge out of sight, and once I see that it's a little more camouflaged, I relax and wait for her return.

Rouge comes out wheeling a travel bag behind her. I think of asking her if she needs help, but think better of it. I'm not here to court her; I'm here to do a job. Not to mention she looks like she can handle it just fine and I don't want to be one of those guys that treat women like they're helpless.

"So how long do you think this will take?" she asks.

"If they aren't too much of a hassle, maybe an hour tops."

"Perfect. I will be out of my show in no time. Should I pay you now or later?"

"We can do it later…I mean you can pay me later." I catch the double meaning and wonder if she noticed. Her giggle suggests she does.

"Slick, Rick. Your girlfriend must find you hilarious."

"She would if she existed." I tell her and wonder why I admitted it. Though there's more I could tell her about my relationships with women, like the fact that I have never had a girlfriend, and no, it's not because I am gay. I assure you I am not. It's a bit more complicated than that, but why should I talk about it? I'm here for a job, not to play love connection.

"Really? A cutie like you. What a shame." She smiles at me and I feel my cheeks burn with a blush. She saves me before I can bumble into saying anything else incriminating. "So, will you be here when I get back, or how do I know it is cool to come back in?"

"Just call the number you called this morning. If it's not a good idea that you come home, I will let you know."

A cab pulls up then, one she must have called at some point and she waves to the driver.

"Sounds like a plan, Stan."

Then she gets into the cab and she's gone. I turn to the house once the car is out of sight and decide to get down to business. It's easier to concentrate now that she is gone and I'm no longer trying to tear through my pants.

Her house smells good, like expensive perfume and bacon. Sexy and delicious; a great combination. I notice how different it is from my house. Where she has chosen to decorate her house with paintings of half-naked women and pulp novel posters to match her tufted couch and tasteful knickknacks, my cramped apartment looks more like a shop of curiosities. My place is nothing to look at, but since I never have guests come over to check out the digs, what does it matter. For me, it's a place to eat, sleep and keep my work gear at hand. There are also quite a few strange trophies I've kept after jobs that I would never want to have to explain to people. To them it would just be weird stuff that doesn't make sense, but to me, each one has special meaning. Call me sentimental.

I move from room to room and can't help but to admire her taste. Looking around at the place and what she has, I can't help but wonder just how much a burlesque performer makes. It's all pretty swanky, so unless she also inherited a sizable wad of cash, I assume it pays well. As it should. If I were a woman and was shaking my tits and ass at a crowd of people that wanted a more tasteful routine than Peppermint or Cherry flapping their beef curtains, I would want to get paid well for it.

But what do I know? When it comes to getting paid for getting naked, I don't know a thing. So I think it would be better to keep my mind on the job at hand.

After I scope out her opulent boudoir, I decide to head down to the basement to see what's down there. The basement stairs are carpeted and don't even squeak. Again I think of my apartment where everything seems to creak, grind and groan. Even my water pipes rattle and moan whenever I wash dishes or flush a toilet. This place makes me want to move and find somewhere better maintained, but I know there is a reason that I live where I do. Best way to stay under the radar.

The basement is dark and feels a bit damp. I search around for the light switch and find it next to a pair of old skis and poles. There is only one bare bulb to light the pretty expansive room, but it is enough for me to see the stack of boxes that Rouge had described on the phone. There is only one pile of them, so I'm sure that is where the creature would be. From my bag I pull out the weapon that looks like a baseball bat and walk over to the boxes, whistling as I do. Immediately I hear something, and whatever it is, it sounds scared.

Perfect.

I kick the boxes and send them toppling over so that it will draw the creature out. I hear a high-pitched scream, the same kind of sound metal against metal makes, and out it runs. Like a cockroach or rat, the thing stumbles out of its hiding spot. Rouge was right. It looks like it's made of shattered porcelain, as though it had found a bunch of shattered plates or toilets and made its earthbound body out of it. Even if the spells on the bat failed, there was going to be some pain in its life very soon. Bat versus porcelain; guess who wins?

"Don't move!" I yell at it and lift the bat. It freezes, hunching close to the ground, terror on its face. "What's your name?"

"Why?"

"Just tell me."

"Daz," it says and stands upright again. I'm not sure it knows who I am or what I mean to do.

"And what exactly are you? Where are you from, Daz?"

"I am a Thanilk, and I am from very far away from here."

"Aren't we all?" I say and take a step closer, perfect striking distance. "Do you know who I am?"

"The male friend of the woman that lives here?"

"Not really, though it does sound nice. No, Daz, my name is Dillon and I'm a hunter. You know what that means?"

At my name, Daz reacts and backs away from me. He knows all right and if I don't act fast, he'll get away. I lunge forward and get ready to strike, bat raised over my head and I'm glad that I am not a cop or someone that has to follow any stupid rules. My one and only job here is to find any creatures in my sector, anything that may have found their way into the Earth realm, and to send them back where they came. Violence is part of the game. They know it, and I know it.

Now I'm sure you'd love to hear that Daz pleaded his case,

or put up an awesome fight worthy of some Hollywood special effects, but there is rarely any of that in my line of work. Usually it's just in and out. Wham, bam; thank you ma'am; and Daz is no different. My bat hits him in the left size of the face and luckily the spellbound weapon does the job that Godfrey promised. Daz cries out and comes apart. There is a sound like ice cracking on a pond and then he shatters and what is left of the illegal creature is just a pile of broken porcelain. Gray mist bleeds from the shattered pieces for a second before it evaporates. That's Daz departing from here.

"Well, that was pretty easy." I whisper to myself, but as I turn to leave the basement, ready to call up Rouge and tell her I am done, I see that Daz isn't alone. At first I hear the clatter of porcelain being shaken, and then see the shadow of something in the corner. "Great."

Close to where the fallen boxes are, there is another porcelain creature that looks very much like the former Thanilkian. I step towards it and hear the sound of sobs. Now despite what you might already think of me, I still have a heart and that sound kills me a bit. Mainly because it is a female, but one that sounds young. Then what I hear makes it all that much worse.

"D-d-daddy."

Great! This is just what I need. Not only do I have two of these things down here, but it's a father and child duo. I hate it when they crossover illegally and bring their kids. I have no idea why they do it. I've wondered about it so many times before. Are they running from their world because it's terrible there, or maybe they owe a creature from their home world the way people here owe loan sharks and they can't pay back the debt? Do they have dreams like immigrants to America once did, that there is some sort of promised land here? That they will crossover and everything will be perfect? And who gets to be the one to break their bubble? Good old Dillon. Sometimes I feel like little more than border patrol for this place.

Despite the tears and the cries for daddy, I have a job to do. There are consequences not just for the ones that crossover, but for me too, if I let one go knowingly. You might not know this, but I answer to people too. We all have bosses.

I say nothing. The little Thanilk steps out of the shadows and walks over to the shattered remains of her father. I watch as she kneels down and touches the bits and pieces of him, but there is nothing left of him there. I feel bad as her sobs get louder and she turns her makeshift face to me.

"Why did you do that? Why did you kill my daddy?"

There's nothing I can say here that will make anything better. I just look at her, holding the bat I used to take her father away.

I have to finish this. I have to hit the child the same way I did her father. I was hired by Rouge to do it, but others are no doubt watching this right now. If I let her go, I won't be Dillon the Monster Dick anymore and they will just send someone else to do the job. I try to think of a positive thing here. At least I will be able to reunite her with her dad. I guess that's something.

"Why did you take my daddy away?"

I say nothing as I lift the bat in the air. Then, the only word that comes out of my mouth before the spellbound wood swings is sorry.

My job isn't always fun.

SATURDAY

I'm sitting in a coffee shop twiddling my thumbs nervously, but I haven't even touched my coffee, so I know it's my nerves, not the caffeine. I feel stupid and immature. I'm usually the definition of cool and calm, but I have been thinking about Rouge quite a bit since I saw her. When she called, she asked if we could meet today instead of her just sending the payment to me, wanting to meet at this coffee shop. I was reluctant, but really wanted to see her again so I said yes.

Now with her about to arrive, my stomach and brain are taking turns on the Hurl-A-Whirl. I try not to think about her, do my best to listen to the bad acoustic music the hipsters here love to play, but as hard as I try to avoid it, I can't keep my thoughts away from her. I start playing scenarios over and over again in my head, trying to come up with ways to sound cool, to impress her and make her laugh. I don't know much about women, but I am pretty sure that most of them like a sense of humour. And I am positive that Rouge is one that does judging by her quick wit yesterday.

Still, what am I hoping to accomplish here? Why is that I want to impress her so badly, since I'm pretty sure nothing can come of it? For one thing, this woman is so far out of my league that it's like I'm a t-ball player and she is a hall of famer.

There's also the complication of who I am and what I do. There's a reason I've never gotten involved with a woman before, and that all has to do with the job. For the most part I think it's not really looked too well on by the higher ups. There are rules I agreed to, and even though messing around isn't one of them, getting too involved with any one person is a bit of a no-no. Some might say that's very Catholic church of us, but the rules are there for a reason. They don't want us to get so involved with one person and then neglect our duties. At least, that's what I'm guessing, though there could be other reasons too.

Still, I want more than just a client payment here. I feel so drawn to her, and unless you've ever met someone that sticks in your head like glue, you'll never know what I mean.

I take a deep breath and tell myself to be calm. I've faced monsters and demons that would make the toughest man cry. Surely I can talk to this one woman; my client.

The door chime jingles and there she is. Oh God, I feel sick.

She is nothing short of a vision. Even though she isn't all dolled up like she was the day before—sporting jeans, cowboy boots and a band t-shirt now—she is something to behold. Rouge moves towards me with grace and confidence, and she must know that every guy is either looking at her or fighting not to. I try and keep my poker face as I stand up, being a gentleman, but she smirks and I know she can see right through me.

"You can sit. I'm not the Queen."

I sit down and laugh, wanting to play it off as best as I can. She smiles at me and I try and think of what to say. Women are like aliens to me; monsters even. Sure I hunt down all sorts of strange beasts, have been nearly killed from time to time, but there is nothing in this world or others that I am afraid of more than women; especially ones that look like Rouge Hills. She is a different kind of woman, both new and strange to me; the type of woman that every man with good taste would go after, but are usually too afraid to. There is an air about her, a mixture of mystery and importance, which makes her even more terrifying for me.

Then I remind myself that I am meeting her here as a client, not anything more than that. Whether I can think of some way to impress her or not, for now I have to stick to being professional. I tell myself this as the waiter comes over. She orders and when it is brought, we get down to business.

"So, was it bad?" she asks.

"Not really. Trust me; I've seen a whole lot worse than those two."

"Two?"

"Yeah. Apparently they both came in through a portal in your basement, found some broken porcelain figurines and used them to create their bodies here. Pretty typical."

"Typical? Wow! If that is typical in your line of work, I would hate to see what an unusual day is. But back to what you said, about them coming through a portal; does that mean more will come?"

"No. Portals show up in random spots. They're not real portals; those are actually very rare. This is more of a thin spot where the essence of a creature can come through. And when one of these things manages to find a thin spot, they don't plan on where they will enter. They just show up."

"But they could?"

"Anything is possible, I guess." She sips on her drink and I see she is stressing out. I don't like the look so I do my best to make her feel better. "If it's any help, I have a guarantee that if you ever have another issue, I come back and will deal with it free of charge."

"Really?"

"Yes." No I don't because you never know if and when something else will find a weak spot that leads them to the same place. As random as they might seem, what would happen if a permanent portal showed up in someone's basement? Since I have never had to close one before, never dealt with a particular creature called a Porter that creates them, I would never offer my services for free until I knew the portal had closed or was destroyed. That would just be too much of a pain in the ass for me to deal with. But for this eloquent woman that I can't stop staring at, I'm only too happy to go back and see her again. If the problem reoccurs, of course.

"I really appreciate it, Mr.?"

"Just Dillon. I don't do the whole mister thing."

"That's understandable. I always introduce myself as Rouge. No need for people to know my real name, right? Guess we have that in common." She winks at me and gives me a smile that makes my stomach shift nervously. "So is this 'work' your way of having fun, or do you ever get away from the dark basements and monsters to shake your tail feathers?"

I don't answer right away. I'm about to tell her that I have no social life, that aside from eating and sleeping. Realising that Godfrey is the closest thing to a friend that I have is also a bit depressing. Do I tell her that I've never been to the movies, or that I don't go to clubs, bars or anything like that? My idea of a life outside of work is watching bad television or reading a book. I want to impress her, so I hold my tongue a bit and shrug. I hear that women like mysterious men.

"Oh come on now, Dillon. You're not getting off with a shrug as though you're too cool for school and can't tell me. What do you do for fun?"

"Not much really." I finally admit. "Guess I'm a bit of a workaholic."

"Well then, I think you should ask me out for dinner on Monday. I have a gig, but after that I could be all yours. Maybe you can even stop by and see the show. It's revealing, but you're a big boy. I'm sure you can handle it. What do you think?"

I'm smiling like a fool and there is no way to stop it. She just asked me on a date. I know I'm new to this whole idea of woman and flirting, but her intentions could be only be clearer if she held up a neon sign that said 'I like you'. This absolutely eye-popping woman wants me to take her out, how do I say no to that? Easy; I don't.

"It would be my pleasure." I say, the words all but falling stupidly from my mouth, but at least I got something out. I sound like some wannabe from Downton Abbey, like I think every woman wants to be talked to in Jane Austin-era speech.

"Well, call my cell around six to make sure everything is still a go, and if it is, I will be performing here." She hands me a flyer for the show after quickly jotting her phone number on it. The high gloss image reads *Flirt and Tease* and has a picture of her on it, nearly naked of course, and of two other woman that are clearly headlining with her. The sight of her, largely bare behind the big ostrich feather fans, makes me sure that I will not miss the show.

We talk a little more, flirting at an all-time high, and I start to feel more at ease around her. That is a good thing, because come Monday, I should be able to talk to her without coming off as an idiot. Or so you'd think.

Fingers crossed.

Of course things could go wrong, I could get a job tomorrow and end up meeting a creature that I've never had to deal with before. But aside from death, nothing will keep me from seeing her on Monday.

And like I said, death and I don't really get along too well.

She leaves and I decide to walk for a bit, heading over to the park to the wooded paths there. My head feels light and I can't stop smiling. This is the best I've felt in years, maybe forever. From time to time I pull out the flyer and gaze down at the picture of her and look forward to Monday. I know it will be great.

SUNDAY/MONDAY

The day is a dull one where I do little more than look through my clothes and try to figure out what I will wear when I go to see Rouge. It's tough job since most of what I own does not scream classy. I feel exhausted when I lay on the couch with a sandwich and start surfing through the channels.

I'm fast asleep on the couch with some infomercial playing in the background when my phone rings. I barely hear it, but some subconscious part of my brain begins to swim up from the depths of sleep to answer it, only to have me miss the call. I curse at myself, thinking that it may have been Rouge, but when I look at the number it's not one I recognize. I put my phone down on the coffee table and hope to get back to sleep when the infernal thing starts to ring again. Same number. I am quick to answer it.

"Dillon the Monster Dick, how can I help you?"

"Oh...uh, yes. I just tried calling and..." The man on the other end stammers, but I cut him off, a bit grumpy at having been woken up at nearly three in the morning. Everyone just expects me to be awake twenty-four hours a day.

"Sorry about that. I was sleeping. What can I help you with?" I say and try to not sound as terse as I feel.

"Well, we seem to have a problem here, and I was recently made aware of your website. This looks like something you might be able to help with."

"Depends on what it is."

"This may sound strange. I don't even know where to start."

"It's fine. I'm used to strange." I tell him when he gives me the usual.

"It seems as though there are monsters living in our lake. Maybe even more than one, I can't be sure."

"Can you describe the monster?"

"Well, it's big. And green. I think it might have had tentacles too, but I'm not sure. Quite a few people have seen it."

"Okay. Now you said *our* lake?" I ask as I start to take some notes.

"Yes. I'm the mayor here, in Innisfil. My name is Devon Fent. Much of our town is on Lake Simcoe, up in northern Ontario. I'm not sure if you've heard of it. Now, there of course have been stories for years about Simcoe Sally, aka Ogopogo, but this is not the same thing. Many people in here have seen it and other things near this whirlpool in the middle of the lake."

"Alright." I say and put my pen and pad down. I'm already dubious. I know all about Ogopogo and the myth of the Lake Demon. I also know that every now and then, Simcoe County likes to do things to boost tourism and one way they do that in particular is by getting out word of the Simcoe Serpent. I worry that they plan to use me to sell some new cabins or vacation packages. Then again, if it gets them more business, it will also get my name out a little more, so maybe I should listen. "I can send you an email with my billing rates and we can go from there."

"Is there any way you could come tomorrow?" he asks and sounds desperate.

I am about to say sure when my eyes fall on the flyer for Rouge's show. She looks at me from that piece of paper, a naked goddess, and I know what I have to do.

"Sorry. I already have a client that I am meeting with on Monday. The soonest I could get out there is Tuesday afternoon."

"We can pay more, if that helps."

"I would love to say yes." I lie. No part of me wants to say yes to him over seeing her show and taking her out on a date. "But I already promised this client full service and I don't want to disappoint. It's a reputation thing. I hope you understand."

"Yes, of course. Send me the email and I will get everything going. I hope that if you become free earlier than Tuesday afternoon, you will come right away. This is not good for business and has many of our residents terrified that something bad is happening here."

"If I can get free then I will for sure, Mr. Fent. I will come straight to the town hall when I get in and meet with you."

"Perfect. See you then."

He hangs up and I immediately go online and start to do a little research on the area. The first thing I notice is that there are no news reports or blog entries about recent sightings of monsters. That, right away, gets my scepticism going. Something like this, where a creature is seen by more than one person, especially one living in a lake, should be garnering some interest. Yet I can find nothing on it.

At least, nothing new.

Yet sure enough I am able to find occurrences every five years or so. Stupid reports and shady picture of garden hoses made to look like a serpent. There are articles showing some kids at a camp close by that claim to have "found" the babies of the legendary monster, but they're clearly only large leeches.

I skim though article after article and find nothing that leads me to believe that there is anything of importance going on up there. But when I get an email from my bank saying that a very large amount has been deposited, I know I will go anyway. Even if there is nothing there, they're paying for my time so I might as well go and give it a look.

Still, I know there is no way I will be going up there before Tuesday afternoon. I will make it to Rouge's show and our date afterwards no matter what. Money is nice and all, but there are other things to consider.

Before I go back to sleep though, I want to check on another idea and it only takes a second to confirm my thoughts. There are a few articles posted online, most of them from local papers and towns news sources from around Innisfil about the financial state of the town.

Apparently, things aren't going so well for them. The big name stores that took a chance there—Tim Hortons, Wal Mart, Starbucks and what not—seem to have closed up shop. They all left when the sugar mill shut down and laid off more than half the town's residents. I wonder how much this has to do with the call from the mayor. They have more than half the place out of work, times are getting tough all over in an already tight economy, and they need to find a way to generate money. What better way than to spark a story, get tourists there.

I feel less and less like this might be legit. But the money speaks louder than my doubts.

I shut the computer off and look at the time. Might be able to still get a few hours' sleep before I need to get up. I shut my phone off, not caring at the moment if I miss any potential work, because I don't want to be exhausted tomorrow when I see Rouge.

If it's important enough, they'll leave a message. I'm sure the monsters can wait for another day.

MONDAY

I wake up close to noon and right away want to go back to sleep. The phone call in the dead of night disrupted my already restless sleep, but I know I need to get some things done before the show tonight. I moan my way off the couch, grab a pop and muffin, and then I'm out the door. No time to change my clothes right now. Not like it's going to matter. Godfrey is not the type to care if I'm a wrinkled mess or not. He's a lot of things, but judgemental is not one of them.

I remember the first time I met him. I had just come to the city and was setting up shop and was given his name by another monster hunter I knew. There was no warning about the type of person he was. I'd dealt with dealers of artefacts and weapons before, but none of them have been quite like Godfrey. Even his shop says a fair amount about him. Dark and dirty with a bit of a mystery. Like the store, you can take him at face value, but there is a lot more than the harsh exterior.

I think Godfrey actually falls into the stereotype of the type of guy that would own a shop of bizarre items though. He's tall and gaunt, with long dreadlocks that I'm sure smell almost as bad as his store does. His teeth are the colour of creamed corn and they almost match his jaundiced eyes. But under all that, he's a good person. As long as you aren't trying to buy from him, that is. He is still a salesman above everything else, so there is a limit to the goodness in him.

43

He has not only ripped me off in the past, but he's also put me in some seriously dangerous spots by giving me fakes. Once I was going toe to toe with a beast made of metal and it nearly got the upper hand on me. Figuring it was a Daarid, which is a race of demons from a place I couldn't spell if you paid me, Godfrey gave me a gauntlet that had a spell woven into it that would paralyze a Daarid with one touch. Only the gauntlet was actually a prop from a movie that had been filmed in the city. Maybe he didn't know the difference, or maybe he did know and gave it to me anyway. That had been a close call and I had serious thoughts about killing him that day.

I didn't of course. After all, there were no other sellers in the city and I'm always in need of fresh supplies. But I did bring it back to him, the shattered remains of it at least, and he said sorry, that he'd been duped by the seller. I found that hard to believe. Godfrey had been selling goods for almost as long as I'd been hunting, so how did a fake like that get past him.

When I walk into Godfrey's today, I'm surprised to see that someone's already in there with him. And from the look Godfrey gives me, he is too. The guy is dressed like a lumberjack trying to fit into his little brother's clothes. Skinny jeans that are way too short, a red and black flannel shirt that doesn't even go down to his belt and a huge, haggard beard with the moustache waxed like the hipster he no doubt is. He's wearing sandals with his black socks and has a typewriter slung over his shoulder like a courier's bag, which only confirms the type of person this guy is. He'd be hip if it were 1890. I stand close by so I can hear them talk, pretending to admire a set of gunmetal bracelets and trying not to laugh.

"I don't know what would make the best gift, but she likes weird stuff. She has a shrunken head, so something like that would be awesome cool, yo." He talks like a cross between a pirate and a valley girl, which amuses me to no end.

It's almost too much. I have no idea why the guy came in here or what made him think he would find something for a friend, let alone a female one, but I am dying to see how Godfrey handles it. This is a first for me.

"Well if you don't know, how would I?"

"Cause you work here. Look, bro, I just need something cool and weird. Like a severed hand, or a two-headed pig in a jar."

"Does this look like a freak show shop?" I hear Godfrey getting mad and I wonder how long it will be before he punches the hipster. "What you see is what we have. Now buy something, or get your bumbarass out of here!"

"Wow, dude. Maybe you've heard of customer service? That's no way to talk to someone that's looking to spend money. You need to take a chill pill and just relax a little."

"Get out!"

"Hey, what…"

"Get the fuck out of my store or you'll see just how bad my customer service can get! Out, before I kick you so hard in those skinny jeans that they split like a tin of Pillsbury croissants!"

"But…"

"OUT!"

The hip lumberjack scurries past me, mumbling about how rude Godfrey is and as soon as the doorbell jingles and he is out, I give up holding it all in. I burst into laughter despite the look on Godfrey's face, but walk over and lock the door just so that nobody else comes in while we talk.

"You think it's funny? Idiots come in here now and then and want to buy crap they see on TV They watch some show and think it's cool to have bones and dead things in your house. They have no idea the power that certain things hold and if I was to try and explain it to them, do you think they'd even get it? What's wrong with people?"

"Well, you wouldn't want to see my house." I say and taper off my laughter. "I think that kid would have found the perfect thing there."

"White people," Godfrey all but whispers. "Why are you here anyway? Didn't I just see you the other day? Aren't you stocked up?"

"I wanted to return this." I say and put the bat down on the table. He picks it up and looks almost surprised to see it. Then again, I do have a bad habit of not returning too many things he sells or lends me. "I also have a job tomorrow though. Got a call in the middle of the night from up north. Pretty sure I need a few extra things."

"Like?"

"I have no idea. It may all be a hoax, but you never know. I got a call that there is apparently some sea monster up in Lake Simcoe."

"Oh no. Please tell me you ain't talking about Simcoe Sally?" It's Godfrey's turn to laugh. "There is no way that's what you mean, right?"

"I'm not sure. The mayor called me and told me that there have been sightings by a lot of people there and since he has already paid me, I figure it's worth taking a look."

"Sounds like bullshit to me."

"Me too, but I want to be prepared anyway. Worst thing that happens is that I waste a bit of his money on stuff here and a bit of my time heading up north. Not too bad really. And it could be great publicity for me if it's just a stunt, right?"

"If you say so. Did he say anything at all about what's there other than a monster?"

"All he told me was that there is a whirlpool in the middle of the lake and a big, green monster with tentacles seen coming from it. He also said there might be other things there as well."

"You think it's a Porter's portal?"

"I can't see how. There's no way that would go under the radar of all of the others. I'm sure I would have heard if it was that." I then think back to a few months ago when I dealt with a Gloudian that had crossed through with his physical form. He had mentioned a portal, but nothing had ever come of it.

"Well, if there is a Porter under the lake, you should be prepared."

"I don't think it's that, Godfrey. Like I said, the whole think reeks of being a hoax."

"What do you need then?"

I hand him a list and he looks over it quickly.

"Okay. Let's set you up."

I watch as Godfrey packs a few items and I start to think about the job. I hope I'm making the right decision. If it turns out to be fake and then it can't do me any harm, but what if what the mayor is saying is true, and Godfrey is right to think it is a portal?

Of course, it could be a creature that has simply come through and made its body up of dead aquatic life. That wouldn't be unheard of.

Then again, there is a possibility that there really is a sea serpent living under the lake. It doesn't seem likely. I've never seen real, earth-born monsters in my time here. There are plenty of stories of monsters, vampires and what not, but there's never been any truth to the tales. I should keep an open mind. But a sea creature?

Most people know who or what the Loch Ness Monster is, but have never heard of Ogopogo. The legend is Canadian and Simcoe Sally is the sweet face of it. In some legends, it's a demonic serpent that not only kills most of the fish in the lake that people would live off, but also hunts down fisherman and boats. When a storm rages, the ancient creature rises though the dark waters and attacks anything on or in the lake.

But if it is Ogopogo, why surface now? What would be the point of being seen and drawing attention to itself? I have no way to know now, but I figure I will when I get there tomorrow. I am curious to see if it is real or just an elaborate hoax put on by a desperate mayor.

"Did you say you're heading there tonight?"

"No, I have plans tonight. I'm going tomorrow."

"Plans?"

"Yeah."

"A job?"

"No. I have…" I trail off, but he smiles at me with his yellow teeth.

"Oh, you have a date. Good for you. I never thought I would see the day when a hunter decided to have a social life. It's good. Have a good time." Godfrey gives me a slap on the back and hands me a box of goodies. I already regret telling him.

The nervousness started an hour ago when I got a text message from Rouge.

I hope you're still coming to see me tonight.

Of course.

Are you coming to the show too?

Yeah.

Goodie! I put you on the guest list so you can be up front. Can't wait to see you, cutie.

When I read that, the very last part, that was when I started to feel nervous. I nearly dropped my phone when I saw it, and wrote nothing for a few seconds. I'm glad I don't have a Blackberry so she couldn't see that I'd read it and hadn't responded. I did finally, but with nothing slick or good, just a simple "me too". Not even an exclamation mark. I want to go back and slap myself.

After that, I spent way too long trying to find something to wear. In my line of work, nice clothes are not really needed, but I was sure I had something that would be good for a date. Finally I went with black pants, a black button up shirt and a red tie; apparently the only one I own. Either she'll like it or she's going to think I looked like a waiter from What a Bagel.

So I'm dressed and ready, and I give myself one final look in the mirror, reconfirm that I can do this, and I'm out the door.

The ride there is a blur of panic and nervousness. I hope that I'm not sweating too badly and then wonder if I remembered to put on deodorant. Did I? I really hope so. I give my pits the sniff test and all seems well there. Wet, but nothing that will peel the wallpaper.

I meet the bouncer at the door and tell him that I'm on the guest list for Rouge Hills. He picks up his clipboard and uses a huge sausage finger to scroll down the names to try and find mine. Looking at his thick neck and pronounced brow line that makes him resemble a caveman, I'm surprised he can read at all. Luckily he can and finds my name. I'm escorted to a seat near the front, and I go to get a drink before the show starts. I hope it will help my nerves.

Once back in my seat, the show starts shortly thereafter, and it is interesting to say the least. The MC running the show is funny in the cheesiest way; using jokes that are slightly repetitive, but it's okay because he has charm. As the show starts woman are introduced and come out on stage to perform. Some of them striptease, others perform bellydancing routines and there's a group that does a cancan. There are also men that strip down, but they seem to prefer to use humour over sexuality to get applause for the most part. Mixed in with the stripping and dancing are rope acts, a comedy duo that tells jokes that are as old as burlesque and even two magic acts. All in all, I'm highly entertained and enjoy the whole show.

Then, the MC announces the headlining act.

"Our next and last performer is a local lady that I'm sure you all know. She has toured the world with her classic acts and acts of class. She is a bombshell sure to blow the roof off this place. Ladies and gentlemen, and everything in between and around; start to fan your face now and get ready for the hot, the steamy, the temptress of Toronto, Miss Rouge Hills!"

Around me the crowd erupts with hoots and hollers. Women and men scream as the stage goes dark and I feel the excitement move through the audience. The music starts off slow and builds up as the lights come up; old school jazz, with a grittiness to it. Then, Rouge steps out on stage, in a tight dress woven with so many rhinestones I'm almost blinded. She has a feather boa draped on her shoulders and as she moves across the stage she give me a wink and blows a kiss. I'm sure there are a few jealous people around me.

She moves with fluidity, her body bumps and shakes in time with the music. She takes off her dress, corset, stocking and then her bra. I wish I could describe how I feel when I see her like that, in nothing but panties and pasties, but I'm sure it would be too graphic, so I will skip it. She looks amazing. There is her sheer confidence in her movements and her body demands attention, which makes her even sexier. She doesn't just bump and grind senselessly; she owns every movement, becomes one with the music. The crowd loves it and so do I.

She dances a few minutes longer before the music fades and the lights go down. She blows a kiss to the audience and leaves the stage to another round of screams and cheers. I join in, unable to hold it in.

My first experience with burlesque is a damn good one. Who knew the Pussycat Dolls and that movie with Cher lied to everyone.

When the show is over, Rouge moves into the crowd, in a less opulent dress, and starts to make her way towards me. She stops numerous times on the way, exchanging hugs and laughs and taking photos with people. I watch from a distance and can't help but admire her. Rouge is like a mini-celebrity. The way people look at her, flock to her side to get attention; it's amazing to me. I've never really understood the whole celebrity thing. How people stand in line to get photos or pay to get an autograph, as though people that sing or are in movies are somehow more important. But as I watch her giving another performer a hug, I kind of get it. She has an air about her, one of importance and unapproachability, yet people still go up in hope of a word or two with her. It blows me away.

Finally she's beside me and I'm back on the road that leads me to a state of nervousness. *Deep breath.*

"Should we get out of here?" she whispers in my ear and begins moving me towards the door. "If we just keep moving, eventually they get the hint that I am leaving and stop coming up to us."

"Okay."

"Okay? Is that all you can say?" She laughs and leans over to me. Her warm lips touch my cheek and I nearly stop, but she pulls me along. "You're so cute not to tell me what you thought of the show, by the way. Usually people can't wait to tell me their opinion, whether it's good or bad. Usually silence though, is not a great thing. Was it that bad?"

"Bad? Oh no, you were amazing. I was…you were…well, the whole thing was so good."

"That's better. Being tongue-tied is always better than utter silence. I would almost think you're nervous."

I laugh uncomfortably and she smiles and reaches over for my hand. She gives it a quick squeeze.

"That is so cute. The fact that I make you a little nervous, a guy that hunts down monsters; I'm actually a bit flattered."

We get outside and people call out to her, yell out their goodbyes as they get into cabs and cars. Rouge walks over to the curb and goes to hail a cab, but I stop her and let her know I brought my car. I warn her that it isn't the best in the world, that it's a bit of a boat and straight out of the eighties, but gets the job done. What I don't tell her is that the reason I chose an old Crown Vic is the fact that it is big and made primarily of steel. That is important because inside the panels of the car, deep in the steel body are spells and anti-curses to protect us both.

Better safe than sorry.

I catch her smile when she sees it.

"Are you sure you're a monster detective and not a pimp? Wow! This car is straight out of some old cop movie."

"You don't like it?"

"I like it just fine, but I'm thinking there is going to be an eight-track player in there or a guy named Huggie Bear." I put her bags in the trunk, and then try my best to be a gentleman by opening the door for her. I can see on her face, the way she smirks as she gets in, that she can tell how hard I am trying to impress her. "Well thank you."

I laugh to myself and shut her door and we drive around for a bit before she asks me where we are going. I nearly smash my head into the steering wheel when she does, because after all the worry and the trying to build up my confidence, I forgot to come up with a plan on where to go. What can I say? I'm a little new at the whole dating thing.

I go to tell her that I'm sorry because I have no idea, but she cuts me off and saves me the embarrassment.

"I hope you didn't make reservations, because to be honest, after a show I prefer something a little more low key."

"Any suggestions?"

"I was thinking we could grab some food and coffee from a drive-thru at Timmies and then maybe head down to the lake. It's a bit chilly, but the night is clear and I would love to just look at the stars. After a show, surrounded by all those people, I just like to decompress and relax where it's quiet."

"Aren't you a bit overdressed for the beach?"

"Honey, you can never be overdressed in my humble opinion. Now let's do a coffee run and get my beach on."

The beach is quiet. Only a few joggers and bike riders pass us at this hour, so all we hear is the distant traffic and the waves as they come in.

"So, I have been wanting to ask since I met you; how exactly did you get into the line of work you're in. I mean, hunting down monsters is kind of crazy."

I hear the question and wonder what to tell her. Should I go with the truth, tell her who I am, or go with an easier, less insane approach. I have been asked this before, usually by clients that talk way too much, but never in a situation like this. My typical answer is a lie; that I was born with a gift to be able to find and deal with these creatures, that I come from a long line of hunters that go after the things we are told do not exist, that are nothing but whispers and legends. It sounds good and they usually stop asking.

I don't want to give Rouge the old story, the bullshit I made up to hide, but a part of me–a very big part of me–is afraid to tell her the truth.

"It is crazy, but only as much as becoming a burlesque performer." I say and try to move the talk away from me. It might be easier to avoid the topic all together. "How old were you when you decided to do this?"

"I think I was seventeen when I first saw some old videos of Tempest Storm and then a few more recent ones with Dita Von Teese and Catherine D'Lish. Before then, I had no idea what it was, but I was hooked right away. I did my first show two days after my eighteenth birthday and it's been quite a ride."

"I bet."

"Nice change of the subject by the way. Curved that one right back at me, all slick like. Guess you know my weakness already; which of course is that I really do love talking about myself. It's the one subject I know best after all. So, is there any reason you are avoiding the question?"

"Yes and no. What I do is not all that glamorous so I usually don't talk about it too much. And as to how I got involved in it, I've never really told anyone before."

"So, ditch your virginity and tell me," she says and I think I would love to lose my virginity with her, only not in the way she is thinking. Since I have never slept with a woman, she would be a great first.

"Can we save this one for another day?"

"So, what you're saying is you'd like to see me again?" she says with a sly undertone. I'm not sure what to say. I'm hoping she likes me as much as I do her, but don't want to come off as desperate.

I feel like a naïve idiot, but there's no stopping now. "Of course. Are you kidding me?"

"You never know. I thought it was better to ask. You seem like a cool guy and I don't know how many women you have to fight off in a day. I also seem to scare men off. Maybe I'm a little too intense or snarky. It could be that I wear my heart on my sleeve or that I love me a good fart joke. Who knows?"

That cracks me up and we sit and talk about everything and nothing for longer than I would have thought. By the time we decide to get going, I look at my watch and see that we spent over four hours talking. As they say, time flies when you're having fun.

I drive her home and think about asking to come in, but I try to be what I think of as a gentleman. I get out, open the door for her and walk her to the front door.

"I had a great time," I blurt out.

"Me too. It was nice to just shoot the shit with someone for once. Usually all anyone wants to talk about is burlesque or my tits. It gets pretty boring after a while. But you're a pretty sweet guy, Dillon. Did you want to come in?"

And there she goes, asking a question that makes me feel weak in the knees. I can see her naked body in my head, and I start to tingle all over. I want to go in; to know how her skin feels under my hands; to see what her lips taste like. I want to feel her breath on my ear and her hands exploring me.

But, I can't. Not yet. Not with a big job tomorrow. Not the easiest thing to do, but I know I have to. If it were any other day, I would be in there in a second. My heart is racing and I haven't even said anything yet. I hope this doesn't make her think twice about me.

"I really, *really* would love to, but I have to go to Innisfil tomorrow for a job. Again, I really do want to say yes."

"Don't feel too bad. I wasn't going to actually let you come in yet. I'm not that kind of girl." She chuckles and kisses me on the cheek. "Not on a first date. Maybe next time I won't even ask."

She winks and then goes in her house, leaving me on the porch with shaky hands and in need of a cold shower. This woman is too much.

I head back to my car and play that last line in my head. I wonder if she means she won't invite me in, or she won't give me the option of saying no. I really hope it's the latter.

TUESDAY

I didn't get on the road as early as I wanted to, and when I wake up I have four missed calls from Mayor Fent. I groan at the thought of calling him back. It's a little past one in the afternoon, so I know I've missed breakfast at my favorite fast food place. No choice then; I make a tea to go and grab a stale muffin from the fridge.

Before I get on the road my phone goes off again, only it's a text message, so I don't think it's the mayor. I check, and smile when I see it's Rouge.

> **Last night was pretty awesome, Dill. Had a great time and I hope when you get a chance, you give a girl a call. I'm not being needy by the way.**

> **Would have never thought that. I will call for sure. Maybe when I'm all done with this job we can go to the beach again, or High Park. Afterwards we can see if you will invite me in or shoo me away like a vampire. LOL.**

I hit send and regret that the last part sounds lame. Not to mention I don't want her to think I might be a vampire. I'm a lot of things, but a blood sucker is not one of them. She responds with a tongue-sticky-out face, which I guess is a good thing. I tuck my phone into my pocket and get on the road.

As I said before, I don't like to drive all that much. But getting out onto more remote roads where there is less traffic, less city and a whole lot more nature; that I don't mind as much. And when I get to do it with music playing—today it's a mix of CCR and The Cramps—it makes the drive that much more bearable.

The drive is pretty great. The traffic on the road I'm travelling is sparse; next to nobody is heading north this time of day. Less than an hour later I see the sign that welcomes me to Innisfil, population 12,153. That's a lot more people than I would have thought. The place is small, even as small towns go, and I wonder if it has been updated since the mill shut down. I'd be surprised if there's still that many people living here since the main source of employment closed. Most people would not live this far out of a major city unless there were jobs. Without the mill, this will just become more of a seasonal town, a place known more for cottages and fishing. But if there are still over twelve thousand people living here, something else is bringing in money. And if there is another industry, then there's less need for an elaborate hoax.

But I'm not ruling it out.

I drive along the highway until I find the main street and turn onto it, hoping to get to the town square and the mayor's office quick. That way, if this is a hoax after all, I may still get home by sundown and can give Rouge a call. I've never known someone that sticks in my head the way she does. I feel like I'm obsessed with her and think that this is how a junkie must feel: a need that builds and builds, that urge for the next fix that makes it impossible to concentrate. It better eventually die down a bit or I have no idea how I'm going to get anything done.

I drive along the main street and there are a few people here that wave to me, as though they know who I am. Looking at their faces, I think that they look like zombies in a way. Unlike people in the city that are usually animated with anger, laughter or insane conversations with themselves, I have always found people in the country or smaller towns subdued. They sometimes smile and wave, but there's a dead look in their eyes as though they have nothing going on in their heads. Not all people are like that, mind you, but a good many.

I wave back and am glad to find the town hall, where the mayor is undoubtedly pulling out his hair as he waits for me. I park in a spot close to the building and as I get out, there are two old women standing behind me, the smell of fish sticks and pee drifting to me on the breeze.

"You're a handsome one," the first of the two says and giggles. "Isn't he Agnes?"

"Very much, Dorothy. A right looker. Best looking stranger to come here in years." Agnes reached one of her spider fingers towards me and touched my chest. I tried not to cringe. "Oh! And he feels like he's carved out of stone."

"Let me see."

As Dorothy steps forward, I move away and hold up my hands to ward them off. I'm not a huge fan of old people. Some people might think it's the smell, or their wrinkled faces, but it's not. For me, it's the straight-up stages of decay of a body as they move through the daily grind. The physical formation of death as it weaves its way into every cell, breaking them down right before your eyes, until their bodies just stop working, throw in the towel and call it a day. That might sound terrible, but it's my own irrational thought and I'm allowed to have it

"Ladies, please, leave the poor man alone."

I turn at the sound of the deep male voice and see a tall, gaunt man in police uniform. He leans on a post near the stairs of the town hall, a coffee in hand and a smile on his face. Finally, a police officer is there when I need them.

"Oh, Hank! You're no fun," Dorothy groans and walks away with Agnes in tow. A few steps away she turns back to me and blows a kiss. I want to hurl.

"Sorry about. Old girls are a little flakey. They read too many of those romance books and think they are still in their twenties. They're harmless though."

"I'm sure," I say as I walk towards him. "Is this where I'd find the mayor?"

"Here or over at Billy's Bison Burgers. He eats and sleeps at both so there's no telling for sure. You here for any reason?"

"I guess I am. He called me about some strange things out by the lake."

"Old Simcoe Sally?" he says, eyebrow raised, and I see his face change, as though he just remembered something. "Oh, shit! You're that monster wang guy, ain't you?"

I smile and wince at the same time. One of the drawbacks of the name is people making penis references now and again. I know that Dillon the Monster Dick isn't the classiest, but at least it's easier to remember, right?

"Close enough. And you are?"

"I'm Sheriff Gibson." He holds out a long fingered hand that looks more skeletal than human. I take the proffered hand and his cold, damp skin against mine squicks me instantly. Feels like I'm shaking a fish instead of a man's hand, but I try and forget about it as he leads me up the stairs. "This town is something else, but I'm sure you'll see that soon enough. Place is full of strange characters like Dorothy and Agnes back there. You see that guy over by the hardware store?"

I turn and look at a man in overalls that are too short for him.

He has a stroller and is rocking it back and forth as he looks up and down the street with a dim smile on his face. He doesn't look so strange to me, just someone a little short on the I.Q.

"His name is Tanner. Lives over by the main trailer park, still with his mom and dad who run it. That stroller doesn't have a kid in it."

"Dolls?" I ask, thinking maybe Tanner is one of those guys that have a doll fetish. In a way, I think fetishes are so broad, they're becoming what would be considered normal. Maybe he had always wanted to be a girl and now that he's an adult he can finally live out that desire. Sometime you just have to follow your bliss.

"Dolls would make sense, right? Or even a cat. No, what Tanner has in there is loads of cabbages. Usually about six or seven heads, but you never can tell. Some days he has less because they rot and he doesn't get a chance to pick up fresh ones."

"Why?"

"From what his dad told me, Tanner used to want a Cabbage Patch Kid when he was growing up. Only problem is, he never really saw one, just heard the other kids talk about them. So when he was old enough to make some of his own decisions, he decided he's getting some Cabbage Patch Kids. Only, he thought they were just actual cabbages that he gave names to. Nobody has had the heart to tell him differently. Seems so happy with them; why spoil it?"

"That seems…"

"Sad? It is, but why make him feel any worse?" the sheriff says.

I totally get it. If it's not hurting him and people don't really tease him, it shouldn't matter.

"Now, there's Nancy over there by the coffee shop. No Starbucks here, yet, but the owner in there, Tom, makes a mean cup of Joe if you ever need it. But it's Nancy there you should look at."

And look I do. She's standing there by the coffee shop in her cheerleader uniform, sipping on her drink and looking very attractive. From where we're standing I have no idea if I am committing a crime admiring her, not sure if she's in high school or college. I push those thoughts down, thinking of Rouge instead and wait for the sheriff to tell me what is weird about her.

"You'd never guess that Nancy there is forty-one and the mother of two, would you?"

"Really?"

"Yep. If you got closer you might, but from here she looks pretty good. And her coffee probably has at least half a mickey of whiskey in it. We've busted her in the past for it, and her husband does his best to keep her away from the kids when she's too hammered."

"Why the cheerleader uniform?"

"Used to be the head cheerleader at the local high school. She was pretty sexy back then, and had quite a reputation. Then, she had two kids and like everyone else, she aged. One day, she starts leaving the house like that and never stopped. We all figure she is just trying to re-capture her youth. Oh great, here comes Preston."

I look in the direction that the sheriff's trying to avoid looking in and see a man in his early thirties, dressed all in black with tactical boots, a bulletproof vest and a duty belt with more equipment than the sheriff is wearing. He has a thin moustache and goatee and a sharp-angled crew cut. He looks mean and serious.

"This is Preston. He thinks he's a cop. He's actually a security guard. Worked over at the mill before it closed and since then works over at the liquor store. People around here have nicknamed him Robocop."

"Sheriff!" Preston calls out and picks up his pace. "Sheriff, so glad I caught you. I need to brief you on some suspect activity in the area by my site."

"Not now, Preston. I'm a little busy here."

"Police business? Maybe you should give me the pertinent info."

His voice that is like nails on a chalkboard. He whines and up pitches the ends of his sentence, making everything sound like a question. He also pinches his face and stands with his hands on his hips as though he is Superman. I already want to hit this guy.

"You new around here, buddy?" he asks.

I just shake my head. I can sense the power trip he is on.

"What's the deal with this guy, Sheriff? Are you taking him in on something?"

Gibson glowers at him.

Preston clears his throat. "Copy that. Can I give you that info now?"

"Maybe later, Preston. I have to take him in to see the mayor."

"I'll call you on my radio then. Just let me know when you're clear."

"Fine," the sheriff says in frustration and we go into the building.

"He has a radio?" I ask, surprised that they would give him one.

"Not one of ours. He bought this monster of a radio that you can tune into different channels on and he figured what our frequency was. We took three of them off of him, but just gave up. He's pretty harmless overall. A bit annoying, but harmless."

"What about the mayor? What's he like?" I ask as we walk down the hall, passing a few people. They look at me, obviously curious, but say nothing.

"Mayor Fent is a good man, but he has his quirks. As I said, you can usually find him here or at Bob's Bison Burgers, so that might tell you that he's a big man, but he's a VERY big man. I'd say he's pushing three hundred and eighty pounds. But he's a great guy, done a lot for this town. We got hit pretty hard when the mill shutdown, but he's managed to keep things funded and running smooth. The guy before him was a bit of a hard ass that was more into lining his own pockets than he was taking care of people, so Mayor Fent is an improvement. Not sure what else to tell you. He is a bit nervous, can seem on edge. Especially over the last few days."

This should be fun.

We get to the mayor's office and meet his secretary, a small woman with big glasses named Sally Anne. She's quick to pick up the phone to announce us and through the door we hear the mayor bellow "Come in, come in." I follow the sheriff into a warm room that reeks of salty meat and onion infused sweat. The mayor smiles brightly at me from behind his paper-scattered desk, assorted fast food wrappers tucked between sheaves of official documents.

His face is red, and I'm not sure if it's excitement or because his heart is working so hard. His eyes are wide and nervous, even as he tries to hold them on me and his face is a sheen of sweat and oil. I wonder how long someone can live in this state.

"Dillon, you finally made it. I was starting to worry. I called and called and called and you didn't answer and I told Sally Anne, I said Sally Anne, I don't think he is going to show up and she told me to relax, and I said relax, how can I relax at a time like this when we are expecting…" He finally stops and nearly gasps for breath. His face becomes even redder and he wipes at it furiously. "Well, when we are expecting you, and then you don't answer your phone, I started to doubt you'd show up."

"Well, you can relax now, Mayor Fent, because I'm here," I say in hopes that he will relax and not have a heart attack on me. He leans back in his chair and his breathing slows. I think everyone in the room breathes a little easier.

"Well, Mr. Mayor, I think I should be off now. Feel free to give me a shout if you need me for anything," the sheriff says as he tips his hat and walks out.

"Thanks, Gib. Will do."

"You too, Dillon. If you need anything, don't be afraid to ask."

"Thanks." I say, glad to receive the warm welcome. It's been a long time since I've had any dealings with police on a job and today it went better than it ever has before. Maybe times are changing. "I will."

And with that, the sheriff is gone, leaving me alone with the mayor and his body odour. What more could I ask for?

"Please, Dillon, have a seat." I do as he asks.

The walls are set in dark wood and crowded with pictures of the mayor and different celebrities. Not sure where these were taken, but I think Fent likes to feel important. Why else have photos of people who have never stepped in let alone heard of the town of Innisfil? More than likely it's so when people come to see him, they get a sense that he's a man that knows people.

I see him in a different way. When I look at him, and the pictures on his wall, I see a sad man that goes to conventions and movie premieres to pretend that he is rubbing shoulders with the stars. I know by the way each picture seems intimate, as though he knows them, in the way he hugs them or has an arm throw over their shoulder. It's to make him seem as though they're friends, when it's clear to anyone with a brain they're not. Still, I won't judge the man. We all want to feel like we're somebody.

"I really was worried that you weren't coming out. I thought something might have happened to you on another job."

"Nope. I'm good to go," I tell him. "So when should we head out there?"

"You want to get started already? I thought you might like to check into your hotel room and sleep, start tomorrow fresh."

"I'd rather get things going as soon as I can. The quicker I can start, the faster I can get done. Then you and the town can rest easy."

The mayor's eyes widen even more than when I first came in and all I can think is that I got him: it's a hoax. I'm pretty sure he was hoping I wouldn't want to go out to the lake until tomorrow so that he'd have a chance to fine tune the last details and have everything set up. They must not be ready yet, from the look of trepidation in his eyes. He looks out the window, and then back at me with a weak smile.

"If you really want to, I guess we could."

"Is it not a good time? I mean if there is something you need to do before we go out, I would understand, Mayor Fent." I say, letting him know that I have suspicions.

"Oh no, that's quite alright, I guess. No time like the present and all." He lets out a nervous laugh and we leave for the lake.

The drive to the lake doesn't take long and that's a good thing. The mayor decides we should take his car and if he ever suggests it again I will say no. The monster SUV reeks of his body odour and cigarettes, with a hint of meaty grease that I can feel clinging to my skin and clothes. Even the open window that I try not to stick my head out of does little to help the sickening odour. He asks if I want to turn the AC on and I tell him no, that I prefer the fresh air. He nods and tells me an almost scripted story of the town and how great it is. I would love to repeat it, but I'm not really listening too carefully, I'm too busy trying not to gasp for air or throw up, but I nod in the right places to make him feel as though I'm listening.

We pull into a gravel lot and as soon as he puts the car into park, I'm out the door and breathing in the unstained air. I feel my strength coming back and my stomach settling as I wait for the mayor to come out and join me, no doubt ask me if I'm okay. When he doesn't, I turn back and see that he is still sitting in the car.

"If you don't mind, I think I'm going to stay here. Not really in the mood for the slight hike up to the lake. I didn't sleep very well last night. I hope you don't mind?"

Right, I think but don't say. "Where am I going exactly?" I ask instead.

"Just go to the path right over there by those birch trees and follow it. It will take you right to the lake. If you stay on the path, you should be fine."

I turn and look at the thin, dirt line that could be called a path leading into the thick woods and am glad that he is not going to come with me. This way I can see whatever I'm going to see with my own eyes and use my own judgement without him trying to influence me. I'm still sure the whole thing is a hoax and that what he really wants to do is call whoever is down by the lake and make sure they set out whatever stunt or poor special effects they have in place. I'm ready for anything at this point.

"You sure you don't want to come?"

"Positive."

"So I'm just supposed to go and find the lake on my own, and figure out what your monster is? Any hints you want to give me?"

"It's all down there. Like I said, just follow the path and then you'll get to the lake. You'll see soon enough."

I turn away and walk into the woods, making my way to the lake.

The woods are loud with bugs and birds. I move quickly through them, staying on the well-tramped path, not wanting to get eaten alive by anything that might be out there. I don't mean monsters or demons, just the regular nasty life of the woods. The things I chase I can handle without a problem, but if I find a spider on my arm, I break down and scream like a child. Just thinking about one of those hairy, multi-legged bastards moving their tiny legs up my arm is making my skin crawl even now. I despise bugs.

How much? Well, because of them I once nearly failed on a job. I had been called by a man that lived in an old Victorian house in the west end of Toronto. He said he had called an exterminator for the problem, but when the man showed up to spray the place, he said there was nothing he could do and gave the homeowner my phone number. When I asked the client what the problem was, all that he would say was that he had some sort of pest in his basement and he wanted it out. I never say no to a job, so I went.

What I found was a Frath, a demon from the Tanjeen realm. When it had crossed over from its world to this one though, it had called forth the nearby nests of wasps and roaches to form a body. As soon as I stepped into the basement where the creature lived, I was overwhelmed by the pungency of vile, acrid bug juices. I turned on as many lights as I could and before long I heard the clicking and ticking by the water heater. As I moved forward, I recognised the dull buzz of the wasps. Even before that day I had an irrational fear of bugs, and that sound sent a chill up my spine. I stopped so abruptly that I slid on the painted concrete floor. That's when it came out and screamed at me, as though ready to attack.

I froze.

Terror filled me as I looked at a creature made up of moving and swelling bugs. I had no idea what to do. I was planted to the ground with fear and disgust, and I guess I was lucky because by the looks of it, the creature was in the same state. I guess it had expected me to just attack, but when I stood in place, locked by terror and irrational fear, it had no idea what to do.

"What are you doing, hunter?" it asked me with it creaking, no doubt speaking through the combined mouths of the bugs. "You are here for me, are you not?"

I said nothing. I didn't move or even blink. Cockroaches of different sizes crawled across the new body of the Frath, and I was sure I could hear their little legs rubbing and clicking as they moved. I watched the flutter of the wasp wings and clenched my fists knowing I needed to do my job but how was I supposed to when I didn't want to touch the damn thing.

"Make your move, hunter!"

I took a deep breath and reached into my pocket. Each pocket contained items to deal with different entities, and I knew that the right, front pocket had just what I needed. From it I pulled what appeared to be a silver dollar and squeezed it in my hand. I would have to be fast, and once the creature was dispatched I knew I would have to get out of there before any of the bugs touched me.

I threw the coin, which is known as an Ardoon, on the ground. The Frath backed up, but too late. The coin hit and the metal sang out with high-pitched sound my ears couldn't pick up, but that the demon heard good and well. It screamed and threw its arms in the air. The insect body quaked, bugs vibrating up and down its false form, and I moved back towards the stairs. Actually, I'm pretty sure that I ran and might have even screamed, swatting at the air even before the demon exploded. In every direction, live and dead insects sprayed the room. A few hit my hands and cheeks and I'm not too proud to admit that I cried out when they did. I guess I sounded like a fool and I was glad that the man that hired me wasn't there to see me run from his basement like a scared kid from a haunted house ride.

That's not the only reason I don't like bugs, so I want to get through the woods before any bug puts its feet on me. Or even before I walk through some invisible web put in my path by an evil spider who just like to see people squirm. Another good reason I should be glad that the mayor didn't come through the woods with me.

Luckily I make it through without incident.

The woods open up and before me is a pristine lake that glimmers in the sun. There is no beach here; just a patch of grass that cuts off into a short bank before the water. I stop for a moment and look out over the lake to see if there is anything out of the ordinary.

I see the whirlpool right away and it's bigger than I thought it would be. It's at least forty feet wide and swirling pretty damn fast. I wonder what the hell the source of the thing is.

There's a beach over to my right. I pan along the shoreline to see if anyone is there—any random person or even someone that might work for the mayor—but I'm alone. Not a single boat on the lake either, which strikes me as strange, but the whirlpool there may deter people.

I don't know too much about whirlpools, but I would guess they would be something like a vortex or black hole; there must be some unpredictability, a sort of pull towards it. I'm not sure I would set a boat in that water for fear of getting sucked into it.

But the whirlpool is only part of the reason I'm here. They happen naturally all the time, so it shouldn't be the focus of my attention. I'm here to look for the monster that the mayor claims lives in the water.

I walk to the edge of the bank, expecting at any moment to see some poorly-made serpent slither out of the sparkling water. I'm still convinced it's a hoax. How's the mayor is going to pull it off? Will it be some silly shadow under the water? I have no idea how much money he might have pumped into this stunt, but I'm curious to see how it plays out.

At least I was until I get to the water's edge.

My heart stops for a second and I feel sick.

I look around and find a stick that might be sturdy enough, and when I find one, I use it to pick up what I have found. It's heavier than it looks, no doubt slightly waterlogged, but I eventually get it up and lay it on the grass. I stand back to look at it, not sure what to think except that it's nothing good. Whatever hoax the mayor could come up with would never explain this, so now I give him a little credit. Still, it's nothing that I would have expected when he mentioned green skin and tentacles. Christ; I need this like I need a hole in the head.

"Whatcha got there?"

I nearly jump as an aged fisherman carrying a rod and tackle box speaks to me from my right. He's approaching and looking at what I pulled from the lake. He's squinting at it, and I'm sure once he sees what it is, he'll freak out. It's not every day someone gets to see a monster in the flesh.

"Is it a bass or a carp? Usually that's all you get around these parts." He's right beside me, looking down. He has to see what it is now, yet doesn't seem bothered or concerned. "Oh. Another of those strange little bastards. They pop up now and again, but they're all dead. Tried eating. Not my cup of tea, but I know people have been coming down to get some. Free food is free food."

I can't believe anyone would try to eat this. Its blue and yellow skin shines unnaturally, and it looks more like a monster than a fish. I've seen one of these before, very recently too. It's a Gloudian. I found one a few months ago in a school, eating underwear and attacking students. This looks just like that one—Hickner had been its name—and this could be his smaller twin, or a child-sized clone.

"People have been eating them?" I ask, not able to think why anyone would.

"Times have been tough here since the mill shut down. People will do all sorts of weird stuff when they are desperate and hungry. I did it more out of curiosity. Strangest fish I've ever seen, but they taste like old, dirty cheese and game meat."

"Has anyone found a live one yet?"

"Nope. Wouldn't want to. Look at the teeth on the bastard. Worse than a barracuda."

"No kidding." *Much worse*, I think but don't add.

The old fisherman says goodbye and leaves me with the dead monster and my worries.

It's not that it's a big deal to deal with the same kind of demon or monster I have on more than one occasion. On more than one occasion I've even had to send the same creature back as it wouldn't stay away from Earth. This is different though. This isn't like those others that are an insubstantial form of themselves. It's a creature in its true form, like Hickner.

I look back at the lake over my shoulder and think about

what's happening here. My eyes fall on the whirlpool again and I think that maybe Godfrey was right. Maybe there is a Porter somewhere nearby and there is a portal to another world under Lake Simcoe. It's the only way for them to come here in their real bodies, and if there has been more than one, there's a portal and a Porter.

A Porter could come from any number of realms. They have a unique ability to act as a doorway between two points. This is a sure way to travel from on dimension to another and still retain your form. The Porter, once found, is fitted with biomechanics, machinery that melds with their body and then they're used until they die. Acting as a gateway it not an easy or long life for them. They live and die in nothing short of agony. No creature chooses to be a Porter; it's a curse in everyone's eyes. Any creature that finds out they have a Porter's ability will go into hiding and fight to the death to not to be subjected to that pain and misery. So to think that a Gloudian—even several of them—could capture a Porter is doubtful. There are some that claim that Porters and their portals are nothing more than myths, but I suspect I have the proof of them in front of me. I now have no doubt that the whirlpool is unnatural.

The fisherman said that a lot of dead Gloudians had been found recently. How many live ones are there still here then? I watch the water for a little while, wondering if I will see one swim out from the giant whirlpool. I have never seen these creatures cross over through a portal before. I wonder if there will be some sort of light show or crackle as the gateway is breeched.

Some other monster is pulling the strings here, something with more power and sway than the simple Gloudians or the

Porter. I really don't want to see what it is that is orchestrating this entire thing, but this is my district. I can't very well run and hide from it, so I will have to find out what it is. Or at the very least, close the damn portal. I'm going to need to call Godfrey for his opinion and hope he has something that can help me close the damn thing.

This has put a dampener on my day. I should have come here with a more open mind, expecting the worst-case scenario instead of thinking that that this was going to be a joke. I should have listened to Godfrey and brought what he suggested. I should know better.

I'm so pissed at myself now.

I'm mad at the mayor too. He made the whole thing sound like a hoax by talking about tentacles. I have no idea why he brought up the idea of some stupid mythical sea serpent, since it is total bullshit. A hoax that wasted my time would be better than this. And even though I am sure there is no way for him to know the open portal and how bad it could be for his town, he should have given me a much better description than he did.

I pick up the body by skewering it with the stick and quickly walk back through the woods, intent on avoiding bug contact. The path seems shorter this time around, probably because I've walked it once, and as I get to the clearing where the mayor is parked, I see that he is still in the car. Napping.

Figures, doesn't it?

I throw the body of the Gloudian on the hood of his car and as it thumps against the hood, greenish liquid squirting from its mouth, the mayor wakes up with a comical jolt.

"What the hell!"

"I have a present for you, Mayor Fent. Looks like I caught the monster for you." I chuckle, even though I am mad at him. "What do you think of the serpent?"

"Doesn't really look like one," he says as he steps out of the SUV. "Ugly little thing though. What is it?"

"It's a Gloudian. Pretty harmless unless they have bleachers to throw at you, or you have underwear they want to eat."

"What?"

"Don't worry. I wanted to bring it here so you could get a good look at it. Not much for the headlines, but you can rest easy now."

"So that's it? There aren't any more?" he asks and I can sense that he knows there are more.

"I doubt it." I lie. "These things usually only come through once in a blue moon and they are always alone. Looks like I solved the case and I guess I will take the rest of my payment now."

There is a pause and I can see worry on his face. He knows that there are more of these things. Even the fisherman did, so why is he acting as though he doesn't want to say anything? I am not the best at reading people, but I'm sure he is hiding something from me. I just can't figure out what it is.

"Unless, of course, there is something you know that you aren't telling me."

"Well..."

"Go ahead."

"People have been seeing these things, live and dead, in and around the lake.. I was told that they are coming from the whirlpool. Quite a few of them just wash up dead as that one there, but a few have been seen running off into the woods. People have seen them stealing clothes from their laundry line in their backyards too. Usually underwear."

"Why didn't you just tell me?"

"It sounds crazy. I thought the idea of Simcoe Sally would make you want the job more. You know, with it being more high profile and all. Get you in the news; more business. I'm sorry. I wanted to ensure that I could get you out here to help us out and get rid of whatever it is out there. I'm sorry for lying to you."

"It would have been nice to know what I was getting into, but I'll deal with it now. Why don't you drive me to the motel? I think I could use some rest before I try and tackle this."

We get back into the car after I toss the body into the bushes. I'm glad to be away from there.

As we drive, I look at the woods and try to see if I can see any of Gloudians peeking out. I wonder how many are already here. When I dealt with Hinkler, it wasn't all that easy for me. They are vicious and dangerous with their razor-like teeth and nails. I got cut up pretty good on that one, but came out on top in the end. To think of having to fight five, ten or even fifty of them is not a happy thought. Things might get pretty dicey, but I should come out of this in one piece. I've faced worse.

"So, are you planning on calling for anyone else? Or do you do this whole thing solo?"

"Solo," I say and stop looking out the car window. I can't see anything.

I sit back in my seat and think about what the fisherman said, about people eating the Gloudians and wonder if the mayor has joined in. He seems like he would put anything offered to him in his mouth. He strikes me as the "can I have seconds?" type.

"So, I met someone in the woods that told me people are eating these things?"

"Oh yeah. I have seen it. Actually, I told some people about it. One of our restaurants actually has them featured on the menu."

"What? Why?"

"Times are tough all over. The town isn't as well off as it once was so if a business can stay open by getting free meat, why not?"

"But you have no idea what those things are, or what eating them could do to the townspeople."

"Seems fine so far. Nobody has gotten sick from them."

"And people are fine eating what is clearly a monster?" I ask, dumbfounded. I would never eat something that was a mystery to me. I don't want to put something in my body that could harm me, make me sick or even worse, change what I am.

"They don't think they're monsters. They think they're mutated fish."

"Oh, even better. Let's eat some genetic mutation or something altered by pollution."

"Don't judge us too harshly, Dillon. The people of Innisfil are at the core good people. They are fighting to stay afloat. You might not agree with what they are doing, but we do what we have to."

Sure you do, I think, but say nothing more for the rest of the drive.

The motel room is small, but seems cleaner than most of the ones I've stayed in. This one is rather pleasant, I'd guess because there isn't a whole lot of prostitution or drug trafficking going on in this place. Too hard to hide what people do in a small town I guess.

I lie down on the bed and check my phone for the first time since I arrived in town. I smile when I see that there are two messages waiting. Both from Rouge.

> **Hope you got to your place okay. Message me when you can.**

> **Busy boy! Not to sound too needy, but I kind of miss you. Weird, huh?**

> **I decide to respond before I call Godfrey. I was a little busy. In the motel now, stressed out a bit, but ready to unwind. And funny, I kind of miss you too. Lol.**

I send the message and then dial Godfrey's number.

"Hey, Dillon! You just saw me the other day and now you're calling. You better be careful or people are going to start saying you have a thing for me."

"Very funny, Godfrey, but I don't have time for jokes. I have a really shitty situation here. I need your help."

"Sounds serious."

"Looks like there's been a portal opened in this place. Someone has a Porter and the place is getting real skin visitors."

"Shit! That's not good. Any idea what it might be? Have you seen what's coming through?"

"From what I can tell it's only Gloudians so far. I've heard from two different people in town that say there have been quite a few of them coming through, but most of them are dead on arrival."

"How the hell would a Gloudian ever get their hands on a Porter? There's no way they would be able to subdue one. Unless it was a child they found."

"I never thought of that." It made sense. For all I knew they might have found one of their own kind to be a Porter. I told him this and he agreed. "Now, I need some things."

"Are you going to swing by and get them?"

"No. I thought you could bring them up here. I know…"

"Well if you know, then why are you asking?" he says, cutting me off. "You know very well I can't leave here. I made an oath, a sworn oath and if anyone found out I left here, I don't even want to think of what they would do to me."

"Who's going to find out?"

"That's not the point, Dillon, and you know it. It's not just the principle of the matter; it's what could happen if I left. What if people saw my true face? No. I can't let that happen."

I think this might need explaining. When Godfrey opened his shop and began to sell goods to hunters, he didn't do so out of a desire to become a shopkeeper. He was sent here. He had broken laws and was given a sentence that would have him working until his term was over. He was forced to take an oath, a curse that would bind him to the store, though no physical restraint holds him there. The issue is, if it were discovered that he had broken the oath, a century would be added to his sentence and he would have to work there well into his old age. And from what he's told me, that is still a very long time from now.

He is also afraid that if he breaks the oath, the spell cast over him to make him appear human, which he is not, would dissipate and people would see him as a monster or a demon. He has never told me what species he is, but I have always figured it would be some creature that wouldn't pass as human.

Still, I have no intention of heading back to the city to pick up the items. I need to keep an eye on things here in case the situation worsens. I have a few of my tools, items I have picked up in the past from Godfrey that should be good enough to deal with random Gloudians.

But in order to close and destroy the portal, I need three particular items. I ask Godfrey about them and he has two of the three, and can easily get his hands on the third in less than an hour.

"But if you aren't coming here, how do you plan on getting them?" he asks.

"Do you have anyone that can bring them to me?"

"I might be able to find someone, but it won't be easy. And you'll have to cover the expense."

"That's fine. Just get me them as fast as you can."

"No problem. Dillon, you need to be careful. I know I come off as an asshole, and you think I am a bit of a con-artist, but you need to watch yourself. Even though what is coming through the gateway seems more or less harmless, remember that only someone skilled can bring a Porter to their full potential. Turning a body into a portal is not an easy task, even if the Porter has a high level of power. The others behind this, have more power than you might think. Be cautious, my old friend."

"Thanks for that, Godfrey. You know I will." We say our goodbyes.

I know that he is right. There is more to this than I know right now. Finding out the whole story is the most important task for my safety. If there is some other monster behind this, who is sending the Gloudians through to act as scouts, then what will happen when they decide to come through? I can't predict what it could be, which is the worst part. It is justifiable for me to have this fear of the unknown right now.

An ominous shadow looms over this case. On the surface it appeared an easy case; close the portal and round up and dispatch the Gloudians. But that will only scratch the surface of what's going on. If a larger, unknown shadow is pulling the strings, I need to find out what it is. Otherwise, there's nothing to say that another portal won't be opened. And then I will have to do this all over again.

Better that it be a one-time deal.

Still, having never dealt with a Porter before, there is a whole lot I'm not too sure about. This should be like any other job, so why am I so stressed out? Why do my hands shake and my heart beat as though it's trying to break through my ribs? I know that once Godfrey sends up the supplies I need, everything should go rather smoothly, but there's a cold hand wrapped around my heart warning me that I need to be on guard. I have a pretty good warning system in my gut and I won't be ignoring it.

My phone rings and the sudden break in the silence makes me jump. I laugh at myself and check the caller display. It's Rouge. Perfect timing.

I answer it before it makes it to the second ring.

"Were you waiting for my call?" she asks.

"In a way."

"You busy?"

"Not at the moment. Trying to get everything here set up so I can get back home."

"That anxious to see me, are you?" She laughs and I join her. It's nice to get my mind off what Godfrey said. I stop thinking about the whirlpool and see Rouge's face and body in my head.

"Maybe I am. You'll just have to wait and see."

"How long will I have to wait?"

"Not sure. I thought it was only going to be a day or two, but this is a bit bigger than I thought. Not like your basement." I don't want to tell her the details, because I would rather just be distracted at the moment.

"Are you hoping that I'm going to be as easy as my basement was?"

I chuckle at that. "Of course not. I am a gentleman, after all."

"A gentleman monster hunter? Sounds sexy." She pauses. "Can you hold on; my other line is going off."

I wait as she answers the other call. I hate call waiting sometimes, even though I know it serves a purpose. But I feel less important somehow, as though when someone asks you to hold while they answer that call, it's their way of saying it might be someone they would rather talk to. I know some people might find that ridiculous, but I want it to be all about me.

While I wait for Rouge to get back to me, I turn on the TV and begin to flip through the channels. No porn stations here, let alone premium channels. Only the most basic of basic cable so I have a choice of news, reality small claims court shows, or drivel that they claim to be kid's shows. I turn the thing off and it feels like forever as I listen to the dull hum of the A/C and the occasional car that drives by.

I walk over to the window and look out. The sun has already set and it's much darker here than in the city. You can make out the stars overhead and it's an amazing sight. I wonder if other people look up at them and feel small by the sheer size of space overhead. I know what's above and beyond this small rock; that humans and Earth are pretty small in the grand scheme of things.

So why do so many beings want to come here? If there is so much out there, bigger and better than Earth, what is it that attracts them? My guess is it's because the planet is off limits. The mere fact that they are told not to come, makes them long to come even more. It's like putting warning labels on CDs. You don't stop kids from buying them because of the label; you make them want it even more. One thing that humans, monsters and demons share is that they all want what they're told they can't have.

"Well, that was interesting," Rouge suddenly says as she comes back to me.

"Good or bad interesting?"

"Great actually. Got a gig. Doesn't pay as well as I would like, but the venue is an interesting one. Never had the chance to do a show there before. It's miles better than getting paid $300 to work in a dive bar."

"That's great news then, right?"

"You better believe it, sugar! I thought I was going to be all lonely here tonight by myself, but now I have something to do. Bad news is, I have to let you go. I need a shower and to get my things thrown together."

"What time's the show?"

"I go on at eleven forty-five, so I have about three hours to get there."

"Kind of short notice, isn't it?"

"I don't mind so much. Last minute gigs you get used to. But I really should run. Sorry."

"No worries. I wouldn't mind sleeping a bit. But text me in the morning and when I'm free I will give you a call. Okay?"

"Better than okay. Talk to you soon."

I say goodbye in an embarrassingly lame way and hang up. I kick my shoes off, and decide to sleep. I strip down to just my boxers and lay on the surprisingly comfortable bed. My eyes don't close right away and as I stare up at the water stained ceiling, the swirling lake finds me again. I can see it, glistening in the sun, moving, a tornado in the water sucking downwards to some unseen breech; a crack in reality. I try to push the thoughts away, let my mind move towards Rouge and the idea of seeing her again; of touching and smelling her skin. But her skin melts away and my hand is on the arm of a Gloudian. I sit up and want to pace the room, but I know I have to fight this off. I can't let my fear take over.

I lay back down and begin breathing exercises I have long practiced.

Deep breath in through my nose; positive thoughts.

Exhale the bad energy slowly from my mouth.

Repeat.

Repeat.

And soon I am relaxed and my exhaustion takes over.

WEDNESDAY

In my dreams I'm unable to escape the fear and unease growing inside me. I toss and turn as the trepidation swells in me just as the moon grows fat and bright outside. In my dreams, I run from creatures with probing arms and hungry mouths. They scream my name and each time I wake up from a particularly bad one, the echoes of their voices follow me into consciousness. I do my best to ignore them and force myself back to sleep.

This is not normal for me. I dream as normally as most people do, but mine tend to be strange or sexual, even mundane at times. Never like this. These nightmares are new and terrifying and I'm finding it difficult to wake from them. More than once I tried to convince myself that it was nothing more than a dream and force myself awake. It didn't work though, and I was torn limb from limb by one creature, only to begin the dream again, and be chased by another.

By the sixth time I wake up gasping for air, I look at the clock and see that it is only half past midnight and groan. Feels like I've been fighting my way through nightmares and restlessness for twelve hours, but it's been less than five. I think I might go and grab a pop to get the horribly metallic taste of fear out of my mouth. As my feet touch the floor, there's a knock at the door. I doubt the mayor would come here at this time, but if something happened, he might have sent the sheriff. Either way, I don't want to answer it, but when there is a second, more anxious knock, I know I don't have a choice.

Hell, for all I know there could be anything on the other side of the door: a mass of Gloudians or whatever sent them here, just waiting to kill me. At least then I'd get some rest.

There's a third knock.

"Jesus!" I cry out and shuffle towards the door. "Hold your fucking horses."

Before I open the door, I look over at the dresser and see my gloves, deciding to put them on. You can never be too safe. I've made a few mistakes that nearly cost me my life, and I don't intend on repeating them.

Once they are on, I pull the door open as whoever it is, is in mid-knock.

"Oh shit!" she cries out as the door flies from my hand and crashes into the wall.

"What are you doing here?"

"Well hello to you too, sweet cheeks." Rouge laughs and leans in to kiss my cheek. She then steps back and looks me up and down and I realize all that I'm wearing is my boxers and my spellbound gloves. I hope my gut isn't hanging out. "Aren't you a sight?"

"What are you doing here?" I ask again.

"I come all the way out here and that's the first thing you say? Boy howdy, ain't you a charmer? Aren't you going to invite me in? Unless, that is, you have company already." Rouge looks over my shoulder and into my room, where there's nothing more than my bag and clothes.

She smiles at me as she gives me a second look from top to bottom, her eyes stopping on the gloves. "You wear gloves to bed every night?"

90

"No. They're...well, it's a long story." I take them off and step aside so that she can come in. "Sorry about all of that. I was sleeping and having some bad nightmares. I was a little disoriented. Come in, it's great to see you."

"That's better," she says. "By the way, nice tattoos. I would have never guessed you had so many."

I look down at my body which is covered in a lot of tattoos, scarification and brands. I didn't get them for fashion as so many do these days. Each serves a purpose. They are protection from demons, monster, possessions and attacks in general.

"Thanks." I don't know if I could explain it all to her without making her think I'm a weirdo. Then again, she knows I hunt monsters down for a living, how much weirder could I possibly be?

She walks in, dragging her performance bag behind her, and sits it by the bed. She then struts back to where I'm standing by the open door and wraps her arms around me in one of the best hugs I've ever had. I return it as best I can, feeling the nightmares fading as I do.

"That's for the nightmare. Better?"

"Oh yeah."

"Good," she says and pecks my cheek again as she pulls away.

She sits back on the bed as I close the door, and when I turn back to her, I try and think of a delicate way to ask what she's here for. I don't want to just blurt something out, but I have no idea why she is here. She had a show tonight and I would have thought coming all the way out here to see me would be the last thing on her itinerary. Yet here she is.

"You look like you have something cooking in your head kitchen, Dillon," she says bluntly. "What's on your mind?"

"I'm just surprised to see you here. I thought after the show you'd want to decompress."

"What show?"

"You said you had a show when I was on the phone with you earlier."

"No, I said I have a gig, not a show. And you, Mr. Monster Hunter, are my gig."

She can see my confusion and laughs. "When I was on the phone with you, the call on my other line was a friend of yours. A guy named Godfrey. He said you needed a few items and wanted to know if I could bring them to you. Of course the pay sucked, but since it would allow me a chance to hang out with you, how could I turn it down?"

"You know Godfrey?"

"Not until today. I asked him how he came across my number, thought maybe you were being weirdly cute and gave it to him in case something happened to you. But he said no, that he had a way of 'coming across things', and my number was one of them. He's a pretty strange dude, if you don't mind me saying."

"Not at all. I agree with you."

This was strange. Though I had mentioned Rouge to Godfrey, I know I hadn't mentioned her name, or given him her phone number. I have no idea how he contacted her. I doubt her phone number is registered under Rouge Hills. Then I realize that I don't even know her real name, and I know it's something you should ask. Is there some sort of etiquette to this? Not only do I not have normal experiences with women, but now I have a burlesque performer in my room and I don't even know her real name.

"Godfrey does have a way about him. Not sure why he would go to you, but I'm glad he did."

"I should mention that there is a cab driver outside with a running meter that's waiting for you to pay him. Sorry."

I open the door again and sure enough there it is. The driver is outside his car, looking at me suspiciously. Probably because I shut the door when there was still money owed and he thought I was about to give him the old Ro Sham Bo.

"How much?"

"More than you'd think when it's only an hour away. Best take your wallet."

I turn back and look at her. And she is blinking at me in a flirtatious sort of way. "Godfrey said you'd pay to get someone up here. I could pay, but that would make me a bit sad. You don't want me sad, do you?"

I say nothing, but she is right. I pull on my pants to pay the guy and see that Rouge was right; it's way more than I would have thought. Damn cabbies.

Back in the room, Rouge has her bag on the bed and is in the process of unzipping it. When she gets it open I see that Godfrey managed to get all three items and I breathe a sigh of relief. This job would have been impossible without them.

As I walk towards the bed to take the items out, I notice she's also packed some clothes and one of them catches my eye. It's colourful; red, green, yellow with a bit of black.

"What is that?" I ask.

"This?" she says and pulls out the skimpy outfit. As she does

I see exactly what it is and I can't help but smile. "Every year there is a Fan Expo in the city, and when it comes, I go out in this little number. Comic book boys and girls go nuts over a girl dressed as Robin. Especially one that pours themselves into this little thing."

I look at the outfit that seems to be missing a lot of material in all the right areas and try to picture it on her. It isn't very hard. I doubt Batman would have got any work done if Robin was built like Rouge.

"I brought it since I figured you are up here doing some superhero kind of work. I just thought you might need a little sidekick to you help out." She gives me a wink and holds the outfit in front of her body. "Think I could stop crime and monsters in this?"

"You'd stop traffic, that's for sure," I say and try not to choke too hard on the words. The room is starting to feel warmer than I would like. "But I doubt it would be very comfortable to fight crime in."

"I would never really wear it out there, but in here is another story. Should I try it on?"

The restless sleep is long gone and now I feel like I could stay up all night. Rouge smiles evilly at me and backs towards the washroom.

"Maybe you should clear the bed off while I see if I can squeeze into this before I squeeze out of it for you. Unless you'd rather…"

"Hurry!" I say, not wanting to wait anymore. So much for romance and subtleties. She closes the bathroom door and I all but throw the suitcase and items off the bed. There is a panic beating deep in me, making my stomach flip flop around and causing me to feel light-headed, but it's fine. The feeling of excitement is blowing the rest out of the water.

I start to take off my pants when I hear the door open behind me and I turn to see her there, in the doorway, already out of her clothes and in the amazingly small outfit. There is a deep cut in the middle, a V-neck that gives me a clear view of her cleavage. I nearly fall with my pants half off, but am quick to regain my balance.

"Ready to see why I'm known as the "girl wonder"?"

I'm more than ready.

I wake up and the sun's up. Someone is yelling outside, near my room. I'm still tired, but can tell just by the light is coming in that it's noon at the very least. I give myself a stretch and look to where Rouge is still sleeping, curled close to me in all her naked glory. I think back to the night before and can't believe it actually happened. For a first time sexual experience, I don't think I could have asked for anything better. It was pretty much a Penthouse Forums fantasy come true.

Not sure how she saw it, but I hope I didn't come off as a rookie.

I quietly get out of bed, knowing I have to get my ass in gear, and get dressed as quiet as can be, but as I am slipping on my t-shirt, I see that Rouge is awake, leaning forward and watching me with sleepy eyes.

"Where are you going?"

"I still have a job to do. The sooner I get done, the sooner we can leave here."

"This place isn't so bad. I love the idea of a quiet country life and all. I always wanted a house where my neighbors were a twenty minute drive away," she says and gets out of bed, wearing nothing but a smile. "And how can this place be bad when we made some pretty awesome memories here?"

She wraps her arms around me and leans in to kiss my cheek.

"I'd give you a real kiss, but my breath has some morning gunk to it. Sorry."

"No problem," I say, as I'm sure mine does too. I do like her frank way of speaking. "Maybe you want to go around town while I'm gone, get some breakfast and shop."

"Shop? You're such a guy. I don't live to shop, but breakfast does sound good. I'm starved after the workout. And maybe there is a shoe store I can check out."

"But you..."

"Buying shoes isn't shopping. It's more like feeding an addiction. And it's as hungry as my stomach is right now." She kisses me again and walks to the bathroom. "Text me later and we can figure out where to meet up when you're done."

I say goodbye, grab my bag and head out the door. I wish I could stay with her, go out from breakfast and walk down by the lake, enjoying the day. But I'm here for a reason and that won't wait for me to go on a date and maybe have a little more sex.

I toss my bag into the front seat of my car and drive towards Lake Simcoe. As I head down Main Street, I pass some of the regulars that Gibson pointed out the day before. All the people in their place; it looks a little like a carbon copy of the day before. I think it's pretty strange, but I have never lived in a small town like this, so I have no idea what is normal here. I know that people love their routines though. Morning coffee, nightcaps before bed, the annual reading of a book or a daily walk to their favorite part of town. People do love to relive things, as if the memory of what's important to them will dissipate if they don't.

I'm about to turn onto the road that leads to the lake when police lights come on from behind me and I pull over. It's the sheriff no doubt. I follow the rules and pull my car over to the curb and watch as the police car does the same. As I thought, Sheriff Gibson steps out, straightens his belt and walks towards my car. I wait and roll down my window.

"Afternoon, sheriff." I say as he steps up.

"Sleep well, Dillon?"

"So-so. You?"

"I rarely sleep these days. But that's not really something we should talk about. I wanted to know how yesterday went. The mayor was pretty tight-lipped when he got back."

I step out of the car, hating the way it feels to crane my neck up him. As I do, my knees groan, aching from the lack of sleep and the workout I put them through the night before. I hate how stiff they've been getting lately.

"Actually, he was pretty tight-lipped with me too. Turns out I did find something here. Something that shouldn't be here. I hear there have been a lot of them lately."

"You mean those blue and yellow things?"

"You've seen them too?"

"Of course. Everyone has. Kids have been bringing them home over the last few weeks. My neighbor, George, he threw one of the things on the grill and tried to eat it. Thought it was a new fish species or something. He wanted me to try it, but I'd rather go vegan than eat one of those ugly things. But what do they have to do with any of it?"

"Those are the things I am here for. They're what's coming through the portal."

"Damn. Are they dangerous?"

"They can be. They mainly eat underwear, the more soiled the better, but they'll attack if provoked. Not sure how they'd react to finding out people are eating them."

"Well, the mayor has been suggesting it to people, believe it or not. He's trying to help out those that are struggling since the mill closed. Still, I'll make sure that George doesn't grill any more of them up. Who knows what kind of diseases they might have?"

"That's probably a good idea."

"You heading back out there now?"

"Yeah. I want to get the portal closed before anything else comes through. Then I have to hunt down the ones that are here."

"Need any help?"

"I think I should have it, but thanks."

"It's a strange business you're in, Dillon. I'll give you that. If you do need any help, just give me a shout. Last thing I want is things getting out of control."

"Thanks, Sheriff. I'll do that."

I get back in my car and he gives the roof a quick slap before I continue on to the lake.

I take a slightly different route this time. I see that there is access to the beach, which will keep me away from the woods and the bugs. With the car parked and my bag in hand, I head down to the water, ready to shut the portal and get out of this place.

The lake glitters and all around me crickets and grasshoppers play music to go with the songs of birds. My hands sweat as I've already donned my gloves. I don't want to put them on last minute in case it all goes wrong. I normally don't like to be negative, but when it comes to an open portal, something I have never dealt with before, I can't help but to be prepared. After all, there are already Gloudians out here, maybe close to the woods, so I had better to play this with some caution, in case they decide to attack.

The sand is white and blinding as the sun reflects off it. I squint as I step onto the soft ground and move towards the water's edge. Shells and weed litter the area and as I get closer to the water I spot a few more dead Gloudians. Some look very fresh, their flesh nearly sparkling in the daylight, while others are in various stages of decay. Animals and bugs have also been to see what they taste like. I wonder if they like them more than the people here did.

I pass by the bodies washed up on shore, stopping a few feet away from the tide line, and drop my bag onto the sand. I look out over the water, and at the giant whirlpool. There's no way I would be able to get a boat out there, and with what Godfrey provided me, I shouldn't have to. All I need to do is set it all in motion and the spells and talismans should do the rest. Once the objects touch the water, the Porter should die instantly and the portal will collapse, if that's what it really is.

Now to get to it.

I kneel down and open my bag, but as I do, I hear movement in the brush behind me, to the right. I pause, listen to the sounds and try to make out what it is. It could just be people from town that have come out to see what I do, but when I hear the low growl with a strange clicking sound mixed in, I know it's not that simple. I've heard that sound once before, the day I killed a Hickner with my own hands. Took the little bastard apart piece by piece.

"Shit," I whisper and stand up quickly, drawing both my regular dagger and the one wrapped in magic and curses, a Tincher. A Tincher, it's a blade used for flaying fleshy demons, ones that come in their own skins or use the meat of animals to make their body. It looks like a knife you would use on a fish, with its thin, slightly serrated blade, but this one also has magic that causes even more damage with each cut. It has power that no Earth steel could hold: curses that will instantly kill some, spells that will torture others and magic to shatter the minds of most.

With my gloves on and both the blades in my hand, I spin towards the bushes and see something small and low to the ground, hunched over slightly as though it might be old or in pain. Then it turns its head up at me and I see the ugly face of a Gloudian.

"Hunter!" it growls at me with a snake-like voice. "You came for me."

"For you and whatever is in the lake. A portal maybe."

"Very good. I didn't think you would figure it out so fast."

"It wasn't hard. Too many of your kind have come through and been seen. A portal is the only thing that makes sense."

"You have no idea, hunter, but you will. Won't he?"

As the creature speaks, there are strange sounds, sounds of agreement, but as I don't speak many of the lower languages that these things do, I have no idea. What I do know is that more Gloudians step out of the bushes and stand in a row before me.

Two.

Then ten.

Then thirty.

A noise comes from the water and I look over my shoulder to see more rising from there too, until there are close to sixty Gloudians on the beach with me. With only my knives and my gloves, I have no idea how I am going to make it out of this.

"You look a little worried, hunter. Something the matter?"

Oh there's something the matter all right, but I don't want to say anything. I know when I'm outnumbered, and by the looks of it, surrounded too. I have to hope that they are slower than I am, and weaker than Hickner was. The thoughts of those bleachers coming at me in the school, how quick he was; I'm more than a little worried.

"I think you are done hunting here," the one acting like the leader says as the pack moves towards me. "Where will you go when we dispatch you? Do you even know?"

"I'm not going anywhere, you little shit! There's no way you and your kind are going to be allowed to stay here. Even if you get rid of me, there'll be others to come and stop you. Not that I really think you ugly shits have a chance. I've gotten rid of your kind before, and I'll do it again."

"That's just what I was going to say," he says, smirking with a sharp-toothed grin.

I'm sure he's never dealt with my kind before, let alone killed any, but I don't like that he's talking to me like that. Not sure where this little slave monster got the balls from.

"Well, enough is enough. Get him!"

I have nowhere to run, or plan an attack, so I brace myself. I tighten my grip on the blades and wait for the first one to come at me. It doesn't take long. Four of them charge, claws up, fangs out. When they are only steps away from me they jump through the air as one. I slice through in quick succession. One swipe, then a quick second, third and fourth. I hear them scream and warm blood spray my arm and face. I see the first one fall, its dark, nearly black organs hitting the sand before rest of the body does. A second one's dead as the Tincher finds its throat and nearly slices its head clear off.

The thump of the third I miss because the fourth is on my back, claws digging into my jacket as it tries to find my flesh. I attempt to spin on it, like a dog trying to chase its own tail.

"Get the fuck off of me," I yell at it in frustration and I thrust one of the blades backwards, nearly slicing my own ear off. As I'm doing this, I see the others coming, but they seem hesitant. No doubt it's because of their dead fellows. They are probably shocked that I've killed not just one, but three of them. I hope it's enough to keep them back while I fight off the Gloudian on my back.

I stab at the creature again, but I miss by mere inches. It opens its mouth and bites into my shoulder. Though my jacket is thick, it is not thick enough to stop the mouthful of razor sharp teeth. There is a pinch, a burning in my shoulder and I wince, but as I do, it's almost immediately gone. And so is the creature from

THE GATE AT LAKE DRIVE

my back. I turn and hear it wailing before I see it. Foam and oil-like liquid bubbles from its mouth as it seizes and at first I am confused. As are the rest of the Gloudians on the beach. I've never seen anything like it before. When the creature stops moving, its head collapses a little, then caves in and it's still.

Weird.

The others seem to have lost some of their steam. They look at the four dead around me, mainly the one that bit me and died, and then finally at me. When their eyes fall on mine, I can see the fear. It's a look I know. I take a step towards the main group and they all take a step back. All of them, except the leader.

"Don't be afraid of this hunter! He is only one and he is weak. Kill him so that it is safe for the others to come. Kill him and we will own this world."

"Come at me and you'll end up like them. Like HIM!" I yell, pointing at the one who bit me.

"Don't be afraid of his false magic and spells. He has covered his body in ink, his flesh is a curse. Do not bite him, but feel free to make him bleed."

I have never seen my tattoos work quite the way they seem to have on the Gloudian. I got most of them to avoid the beings I fight from entering my body; more of a protection than an offensive weapon. But it'll work.

"Grab rocks! Use your claws! Tear him apart. And then everything in this world will be ours."

I've had enough. These little bastards are scared and the mouthy one has a chance of making them think they can win. So I do the one thing I know to do: I charge at the leader. Screaming like a maniac, bloody knives raised, I slice the Tincher across his throat before he can react, while I stick the dagger in his chest. His hands shoot up to his open throat and he tries to keep his head from detaching. While his hands are busy with that, I quickly yank the knife downward and all but split him in two. As the dagger exits from his lower half, I turn to the closet Gloudians and kill them too. From there, it gets bloody.

I cut and disembowel, behead and blind. I'm warm and sticky, gritty from the sand that's glued to me with blood. Time moves in slow motion and each time I strike or get hit, I can hear flesh splitting and blood spraying. My own blood runs down my face, down my back and pools in my shoes. They hit me with stones, driftwood, tear at me with their claws. I have no time to feel the pain. If I stop fighting, they will overwhelm me and I'm done. So I butcher them as I am cursed in a language I can't understand. Some of them beg for mercy as I grab them, digging my thumbs deep into their eyes and then into the foamy brain matter in their skulls.

Despite the earlier death, a few still take the risk and sink their teeth into me. It's like fire exploding through my nerves as their teeth break through my flesh and find muscle. I count myself lucky that they can't tear away chunks of me. Though I have no idea which curse it is that causes the Gloudians that bite me to melt and die, I'm glad for all the protection I've covered my body with.

Two large one come at me, one with claws barred, the other with a branch in one hand and a rock in the other. The latter is more of a threat, so I meet him half way. He swings the branch first and the weak wood of the pine does little to hurt me. Before he can try and strike me with the rock I take the Tincher and bury it in his ear; twist it back and forth before I pull it out, along with part of his skull. He falls to his side and I quickly turn on the one that is looking for some hand-to-hand combat. He's slower and doesn't have a chance to avoid the dagger as I pierce his forehead, holding him still while I behead him with the other blade. I'm quick; he doesn't even get a chance to cry out before his head is freed from his body.

More come, falling as the others did. Some get a few strikes in; most don't. More run as the beach becomes a grave for their brothers and sisters, but I don't stop. Some of them I chase, to ensure I won't have to find them later. I fight as hard as I can, pushing away the darkness that wants to engulf me from the loss of blood. I won't let them win.

I can't.

There's no stopping me. I keep fighting and killing, getting cut and bleeding a whole lot. I feel like a machine.

I think I'm done as I pull the dagger out of one of their now empty eye sockets, but as I do, I'm hit from behind, right in the spine. The pain shoots up and down my body, makes my left arm tingle, and when I turn I see one lone Gloudian there. It's holding a rock in its hand, probably similar to the one that it hit me with and I move towards it, thinking of how bad I'm going to make it scream.

"Long time, no see, Dillon," he says.

I know that voice. "Hickner. Fancy seeing you here. I thought I killed you."

"You killed my old body, but there was another waiting for me when I got back. And now I'm here to watch the end of it all. Here to see you die."

"Oh, I ended it all, alright. Not sure about the dying part, at least on my end. And now I'm going to shut the portal."

"Really?" He laughed and played with the rock, tossing it in the air. "And how do you plan on doing that?"

"I have a way."

As I say this, I realize he is standing where my bag is; or should I say was. It's gone now, which means there is no way to close the portal on this end. At some point during the fight, one of the little shits must have taken the bag. Now, unless I can get a hold of Godfrey and get him to get me the three things I need again, there's little I'm going to be able to do to stop the portal from staying open and more Gloudians coming through. This day just keeps getting better and better.

"I think you mean you had a way. Face it, Dillon, it's over. There is nothing left for you to do, but die. Then the master will come through and claim this pathetic world. As he should."

"What master?"

"No time for this. You don't really need to know anyway. You won't be here to see him. You'll be long dead. That's what he wanted."

And with that, he throws the rock at me fast as a major league baseball pitcher and I only have a split second to react. Even in my state, weakened by the fight and the blood loss, I manage to bob to the side and it misses my face, but clips my shoulder hard enough for me to drop the dagger. Luckily, I still have the Tincher. A weapon that Hickner should remember all too well as it's the very instrument I used to take him apart the last time he came to Earth.

I run at him and he knows what's coming; no doubt remembering the last time in the boy's change room. But this won't be the same, as I don't have the patience to take him apart the way I would like to. I would love to skin him and slowly cut each limb of, joint by joint, but I'm in no shape to drag it out.

He runs towards the lake, and although he's fast, my longer legs get me to him before he can dive into the water. I grab him by the throat; the gloves make him wail in agony. I spin him towards me, wanting to look at him when I slid the blade between his lips, push it up into the roof of his mouth and end his journey. But before I can stick him he holds his hands up and starts to speak.

"Please, please. Don't kill me this way again," he pleads and I can see he is near tears.

"Why not?"

"If you do, I'll just go back there again and I will be put into another body and sent back here. They'll do it again and again. I would rather die than be forced to go back. Don't use the blade. Use something of this world so I can stay here in death. Don't make me go back."

"Who is doing this? Who is sending you?"

"His name is Rector. And he is a Hellion."

"A Hellion? There hasn't been one of those in over a thousand years."

"I swear, that's what he is. He is a true demon and he has others with him. Low-level demons and monsters that he has recruited. He is the one that found the Porter. He sent us here as scouts to find what he needs and to kill you. For some reason, you worry him and he won't crossover until you are gone."

"What's he worried about?"

"How would I know that? I'm nothing more than a slave to him. The Gloudian are expendable. He doesn't care how many die, as long as you die. He will just keep sending more until then."

"So, I have to close the portal. I need my bag than. Where is it?"

"One of the others took it. I have no idea. Some of the others think that Rector will give them a place in his army, that we'll have a future. The Gloudian have never had a future. We have always been slaves to others bigger and more powerful than we are. You think you're doing a good thing here, don't you? You find the ones that have managed to escape the worlds they're in, and you just send them back. You never really listen to how bad it is, how much more there is for us here. You are lucky to be here, but I doubt you appreciate it the way we would if we were allowed to stay."

"And if I let them stay, listen to everyone's sob story and didn't follow the rules, follow the laws, they would take me out and replace me with someone else. So who cares?"

"That's just it. Who cares? Maybe just this once you will. I know you're going to kill me, but please, not with that knife. Not with the Tincher or any other weapon you might have that is made to take us away from this world. Give me a true death. Allow me to die here so that I don't end up in a jar again until they find me a new body and send me back. It's hell."

"Why would I do that?"

"Look around you. Haven't you wondered why there are so many that have drowned?"

I look around the beach and have to admit, I hadn't given all that much thought to it. I had just assumed that it was hard it was on them coming through the portal. I imagined that since they are smaller with generally weaker bodies, the Gloudians just didn't take to it as well other species would.

"Better to die by your own hand than to live under someone's thumb. You killed me once; you can kill me again. Only this time, please do it my way?"

I nod and put the knife away. He looks pathetic, no threat any longer. I take off my gloves and watch as he walks to the water.

"I'll go face down so that I don't fight back, accidently scratch you or anything."

"Okay."

"And, Dillon, thank you. It's better this way."

When he lies face first down in the water, I put my right hand on his head and my left on his back. He goes under all the way and after a few seconds he begins to struggle. I look around the beach, not wanting to look down as he fights against the water he is swallowing, the life drowned out of him. I've killed my fair share of living things in my life, but not this way. I don't kill because I like it or from a morbid fascination with the process; I do it because that's my purpose.

But this, killing Hickner in this manner, there's something so pathetic about it that I can't help feeling sick. There's something wrong here; it's more like murder. Killing like this makes me feel like there's a shadow going over my very soul, but I promised him I would. No matter how it makes me feel.

So, why I care at all? When I go after a monster, a demon, some creature that has no right to be in this world and take them out, I'm not killing them in the way most people think. I am not snuffing out their lives the way a bullet would simply kill a human. What happens when I do my job is I send them back to wherever they originated from. Even when I took Hickner apart the last time I saw him, he didn't actually die. But holding him under the water until I feel the last of his struggles drain away, knowing that when I let go he will be dead and gone; that is not something I want to live with. I may be messed up, but I try not to be a real murderer.

When it is finally done, I let him go and watch as he floats away, his corpse floating out toward the whirlpool. I feel bad for him. I can't help but to wonder how bad his life must've been that he actually begged for a true death.

There are other dead Gloudians out on the lake, some washed up on the shore on top of the ones I sliced up. But none seem sadder and more of a shame than Hickner. Perhaps it's because of our past, but I feel like crap. I turn away towards the blood soaked beach littered with the dead. It looks like a war zone.

I walk out of the lake and as my feet touch the sand, I feel dizzy. I look down and I'm soaked with blood, most of it my own. My arms and chest, stomach and legs are cut and there is still blood running down my face and back in thin streams. I need to get back to the motel, clean up and rest. I hope I can drive back before the blood loss gets too much and I black out. It would really suck to have survived all that only to die in a car crash.

I stumble across the sand, thinking again how bad the situation is without the bag. I have no idea what I am going to do without those things, how I will ever close the portal. The last thing I need is a Hellion crossing over to this world and bringing forth whatever it decides to bring. They are bad enough alone, but I doubt that the Gloudians are the only soldiers in his arsenal. Hellions are the very worst kind of demon; vicious, powerful and hungry to conquer anything and everything. The last Hellion that invaded a world left none of the inhabitants alive and within a year the planet was a dead ball of fire. And that one was alone. With an army, no matter how big or small, it could be Armageddon for this place.

I make it to my car, stopping every few steps on the way, fighting off the darkness that is threatening to overwhelm me. Once I get the door open, I throw my gloves and knives on the passenger seat and get in. I start the car and lean back. I just want to clear my head a bit before I drive…

A knock at the window startles me and I nearly scream. The sun is going down and it's odd because it was early when I got to the beach. I realize I must have passed out. Standing outside the driver's window, Sheriff Gibson looks concerned. I roll down my window.

"Sorry, was I speeding?" I try to laugh, but it's weak.

"Jesus Christ, Dillon! You look like you're going to die."

"That bad?"

"You're white as a ghost and no wonder. You're sitting in a pool of blood."

"Had a rough day. What are you doing here?"

"Never saw you come back to town and I got worried. Let's go; we need to get you to the hospital."

"No need. I just need a bath and some rest. Trust me."

"I've been doing this job long enough to know when

someone needs a doctor, and you look like someone backed over you with a lawn mower. You need to go to the hospital."

He's very persistent, but I won't go. I can't tell him why, so I hope he won't force me. I sit up, my back partially sticking to the seat, the coagulated blood acting like glue. I groan. I can hear myself, almost as though it's someone else making that sound, not me at all. There is a detachment there. Not a good sign.

I turn my face back up to Gibson and try to smile. "Look, I can't go to the hospital. I just need to get back to my room. Everything I need is there."

"Well, I'm not going to let you drive. There's no way you'll make it in one piece."

I nod; he's right. The world darkens around the edges and I know that's the blood loss. He opens the door and helps me out.

The next thing I know I'm in his car and he's driving me to the motel. At least I hope he is. I lean back and watch the passing trees as night starts to get a hold over on the day. I'm so tired.

"So what the hell happened back there? I saw the beach. Is it over?"

"Not even close. But I did manage to learn what's going on."

"Are you going to be able to fix things here?" he asks and I say yes, except my mouth doesn't move, and no words come out.

He pulls over to the curb and leans over me. I feel him checking the wounds and as he opens my shredded shirt, his hands pause. "What the fuck?"

"Is it bad?"

"I'm not looking at the wounds. I'm looking at...what the hell am I looking at?"

I know what he sees. The tattoos, the brands; everything I

need for otherworldly protection. For the most part at least. Or maybe he sees something else that is unusual about me. I don't have the energy to look down.

"Later," I whisper and blink.

The next thing I know I am being helped out of the police car and taken to my motel room. I whisper to him that the key is in my pocket, but as he starts to fish it out, the door flies open and Rouge is there, gasping and crying out my name.

"Who are you?" Gibson asks and when I look up, I can't help but smile when I see she is in the Robin outfit again. I guess she had plans on surprising me when I came back, but looks like I have surprised her more.

"I'm Dillon's friend. I take it you're the sheriff?"

He nods.

"What happened to him?"

"Damned if I know. He won't go to the hospital. He said he can fix himself here."

"In this state? Jesus! He needs to go to the hospital."

"No." I say with as much force as I can muster. I try to stand, in a poor effort to show that I'm not as bad as I look, but I'm pretty sure I'm not fooling anyone. Still, I can't go to the hospital. "I have what I need here to fix this. They don't."

"Can I help?" she asks.

"Yeah. Go fill the tub with cold water. Then go into my bag and you'll find a green bottle with a gold cap and a bag of coarse salt. Put three spoons of the bottle in, then one spoon of salt." My words are laboured and I am panting through them, but Rouge nods and gets it done.

The room seems darker than it should. Things are not good.

My body is getting colder the longer I stand there and Gibson says nothing, just watches me with concern. I hear the water shut off and seconds later, Rouge is rushing to me.

"Now what?" she asks.

"Help me to the bathroom." She slides under my arm and supports me to the bathroom. Once I'm inside, I turn to her. "Now I just need some privacy and some time. This may take a while."

"How long?"

"Five to ten hours. Depends on how serious the wounds are."

"Can't I come in and sit with you?"

I want to say yes. More than anything I would love for her to be at my side through this so that she can see that it will be fine, so that she doesn't have to worry. I can't though. Not only do I not want her to see me like this but I can't answer the questions she will have after it's all over. It's not something people normally see. I don't want her to see what Gibson did, or more.

"I can't let you do that. But thanks for offering."

"Well, I'm going to stay out here. You call me if you need me."

"I will. But don't worry, I've been in worse shape before."

"Yeah, well, it's still messed up. And if you aren't out of there when you say you'll be out, I'm going to have the cop kick the door in."

"I'll do my best."

I shut and lock the bathroom door, strip off my clothes. They peel off, making a tearing sound because the blood has sealed them to my skin. I drop them into a pile and ease into the icy water. It bites me with freezing teeth. The bath is so cold and the mix is so strong that it feels as though I'm on fire. I wince, pushing on and get fully into the bath. Then I submerge myself, my head under the water and I close my eyes.

I do the only thing I can do at this point.

I sleep.

M y dreams are dark and full of fear and pain. There are memories of my old life, before I came to this part of the world. Those days are long ago, but in my unconscious state, the regret and dread are still so fresh. A terrible sense of loss.

I'm moving sporadically through time, to my early life as a hunter. Monsters everywhere, wishing me dead, attacking me, and I cry out in fear and pain. Things in the shadows, creatures that once terrified me, and a few that nearly killed me. The walls I pass swell with dark bugs that fly at me whenever I get close. Some talk to me, whisper my name and tell me to come to them. I'm half aware that this is only a dream, but the other half of my consciousness tries to rationalise how it could be happening, convinced that it's all real.

Among the bugs and the monsters are a few friendly faces, but they are few and far between the enemies of my life's work. Most are people I once knew, long dead now, and sorely missed. Their ghostly faces bring nothing but sorrow. They turn their backs on me when I call out their names or dissolve into pools of green and crumbling black rot. I move away from them, my head swarming in a feverish state and pray this nightmare ends soon.

I get a staggered, strobe light effect of my past. Bits and pieces of things I have done, memories that stand out. More than once I am haunted by Hickner's pitiful face as he begs for death. And as he does, the words come to me about what I am now facing.

A Hellion.

A portal from a world where one of the last of its kind lives, into this world, and I have no idea of what to do. I can see my own fear personified. It looks like a shadowed version of myself, hunched in a corner, crying, fear in its white-glowing eyes. I've never been afraid like this before.

I know why. I have never come so close to facing a true demon, a monster of legend like this. I can't think of how I will come out of this alive.

Hickner said that Rector wants me dead before he crosses over. Why? Why not come through and fight me head on? Why send an army of slaves to fight me?

It doesn't make sense.

THURSDAY

I rise from the water and breathe in the washroom's stale air. The door is still locked. Light floods under from the bottom of the door and recognise it as daylight. I slept longer than I thought I would.

I get out of the tub and put on a bathrobe. Looking down at my body, everything is as it should be. Not a scratch or scar in sight. I open the door to see Rouge asleep on my bed, snuggled under the covers and Gibson passed out in a very uncomfortable chair. I'm surprised that he stayed.

He's the first to wake up.

"You're out," he says and stretches. He moans and the way he moves suggests he is stiff and sore.

"Yeah."

"And looking like nothing happened." He stares at me and I know he must be a bit shocked by the lack of injuries. "What's in that stuff?"

"Everything I need. Why are you still here? Don't you have a wife to get home to?"

What I've said is wrong, because his face darkens. I had seen his wedding ring so I'd assumed he was married. Obviously I was wrong.

"She...she's not really around at the moment."

"Sorry, I had no—"

"Don't worry. It's not your fault."

"I appreciate you staying. I'm sure it made her feel better too."

He looks over at Rouge who is still asleep and smiles.

"She was really worried. Seems like she cares a lot about you."

"Really?"

"She cried a lot at first. Kept asking if I thought you'd make it. I told her you would, even though I had more than a little doubt. You were in pretty bad shape. Thanks for not making a liar out of me."

I chuckle and sit on the edge of the bed.

"Have you two been a couple long?"

How do I answer that? Are we a couple? Are we dating, or is this just a fling for her? I have no experience in this area so I don't know what to say or to think. Sure, I've seen movies; I know what love and dating is like there, but that isn't reality. People don't meet and fall in love one day or start dating right away. Or do they? I have some pretty powerful feelings for her, ones that aren't only lust-related, but is it a two-way street? Who knows? I certainly hope this is more than just a fling.

"Not that long," Rouge says from behind me and I turn as she sits up in bed. "But long enough that I'm more than happy to see you're okay, Dillon."

She moves down the bed to hug me. Hard. I return the favour.

"I didn't think I was going to see you walking again." She looks me up and down. There's a look on her face that pretty much matches the one on Gibson's moments before. "How the fuck is this even possible? I don't see a mark on you."

"It's what you put in the water for me."

"Well someone should sell that shit on the open market." She laughs, but there isn't that much humour in it. I guess she's still terrified by the state I was in before. "I really thought you were going to die in there. The sheriff had to keep me from kicking in the door once or twice."

"More like an even dozen," Gibson laughs.

"I had to remind myself that you're not like most guys. Hell, you're a damn monster hunter, so I thought you must know what you're doing. It just took a while to sink in."

"I'm fine. Physically at least."

I think back to the dreams, the questions that came up. I'm worried about what comes next. I have to call Godfrey, since he's the only one that knows anything here, but when it comes to this, even he might be at a loss. If I had access to my apartment right now, I would be able to contact others that might not, but I can't risk leaving town and letting the Hellion get out. Still, I may need to call Godfrey if I am going to get replacement tools for closing the portal. He's not going to be too happy to hear what happened.

"So, what now?" Gibson asks.

"Before anything, I need to eat. Any suggestions?"

We pull to a stop outside of Tom's coffee shop and I recognise some of the faces already there. Tanner's out front with his stroller full of what his Cabbage Patch Kids and Nancy sips on her spiked coffee, flashing her legs at anyone that will look. Rouge shoots me a confused look and I tell her the stories that Gibson told me the day before. When she hears them, she doesn't laugh. She looks concerned.

"That's so sad. Both of them," she says before we get out of the car.

"It's not really. Just quirky," Gibson tries to explain, but Rouge shakes her head.

"It's not, though. She's stuck in the past, so unwilling to accept who she is now. She drinks because it takes away her wrinkles and she can see the person she used to be. It's so sad to see her cling onto the past; that she can't accept who she is.

"And him, Tanner, that's even worse. Why won't anyone tell him? Instead everyone laughs behind his back, call him a simpleton no doubt. He might be embarrassed if you told him the truth, but at least people won't be laughing at him anymore."

We sit quietly for a second, letting Rouge's words soak in. I can see the sheriff is feeling a bit of guilt, probably never seeing it that way. I know I'm feeling like a turd for laughing.

"Sorry, Sheriff. I'm not trying to be a bummer or stick my nose into the way this town is, but I used to be like these people. In a way."

Rouge is silent for a moment before she continues, "When I was in high school I'd dress in Regency clothes and carry my Jane Austin's around. I had this way of talking and it made me a spectacle among my peers. People used to laugh and point at me, called me a freak for being different. Nobody told me that high school would be easier if I conformed to what people thought was normal. And even though I am pretty sure I wouldn't have changed, that being that way and getting treated poorly made me who I am today, it would have been nice to have that knowledge."

"Don't I feel like a jackass," Gibson says and tries to smile.

"Sorry, but I'm not one to keep things in. Let's go in and I'll buy you both a coffee."

At that we get out of the car and go in to get some food.

The bell jingles over the door as it should in a small-town, mom-and-pop coffee shop. The place smells amazing and decorated to feel like a warm, cozy cabin. It succeeds in spades. Gibson tells us to sit down, that here they come over to take your order, and we pick a booth by the window.

Within a few minutes, Tom, the owner, comes over and shakes Gibson's hand. Tom is a burly man, looks more like a lumberjack than an owner of a coffee shop. His wild hair and a full beard would make Santa jealous.

"Nice to see you here so early, Sheriff. Betty hasn't baked any pie yet, but there are fresh donuts, muffins and danishes. Also, we just got a shipment of eggs from the Bates farm if you want some fresh scramble. I'd..." He chokes a little as he tries to speak. He doesn't actually look all that well, maybe a touch of the flu judging by how green his skin is and how he's sweating. "Sorry. Got up on the wrong side of the bed today, but don't worry, my wife's doing the cooking. Like I was saying though, I'd offer to make an omelette or fried eggs, but in the end they'll just end up scrambled, so that's all I offer anymore."

"Thanks, Tom. I think I will get some eggs and a coffee. Toast too. Dry. If you want I'll go give the order to Betty. Maybe you should take a seat."

"No way, Sheriff. I've never missed a day of work and I'm not going to start now. So what can I get you folks?" he asks as he turns to us.

I look down at the menu and try to decide: just a coffee and two donuts or eggs? I could use the sugar more than the protein, but I don't want Rouge to think I'm a sugar junkie. In the end I know I'll get the donuts so as I'm about to order a coffee and two honey cruller, I look up at the man and then stop. He doesn't just look sick, he seems totally zoned out. There's a strange look on his face as he stares at me; mouth hangs open, eyes seem glazed. He looks like a stoner.

"Don't I know you? I think I do. I'm sure I know you from somewhere, but where, because you don't live in town," he says, his voice different from before. I'd say distant, but it's more than that. I can't put my finger on it.

It's just that the man is feeling ill. Nothing sinister, I try to convince myself.

"I get that a lot. I must look like someone you know." I say, for some reason I don't want to mention the website, which is how most people who think they know who I am recognize me. Better to leave it at that and do the guy a favour than to maybe have the sheriff wonder why Tom the coffee guy was on a monster dick website.

"No. That's not it. I'm sure I...I think I know you." Tom turns his head slightly; looking like a confused dog, then lets out a huge and terrible smelling burp. It reminds me of a toilet left unflushed for too long.

"Sorry," he says, but doesn't seem the slightest bit embarrassed. "I'll go get the food."

I watch as he shuffles off, mulling over that he seemed to become a different man in mere moments. Gibson also looks concerned; I wonder if he's thinking the same thing that I am. Mainly that we should get the hell out of there.

122

"How is he going to go and get me food when he didn't even ask me what I want?" Rouge asks. I look at her and she doesn't look weirded out at all by the man's demeanor. "I was going to ask for some eggs too. I haven't had scrambled eggs in ages."

"I don't think it matters," I whisper, moving my chair back. "I think we might want to find somewhere else to eat. Is that normal for him, Sheriff?"

Gibson says nothing, but his eyes are trained on the kitchen and he is scowling. I'm not sure if he is angry or worried. I give the table a quick knock and snap him from his daydream. He turns to me, his face pale and strained.

"What was that?" he asks.

"I think we might want to try and find somewhere else to eat. What do you think?"

"Did he seem a little weird?" Gibson asks and turns back towards the kitchen. "I know you guys don't know him, but he went from being fine to a space cadet. What's that all about?"

I have no idea what could be wrong, but Gibson's concern makes me worry. There's already happenings in this town that have me on edge, too many things that shouldn't be, so I know that this might be connected. I want to get out of here ASAP.

"Look," I start, "whatever it is, I think we can all agree that it's not normal and probably won't be good. So as fast and as calmly as you can, we should get up and get out of here. Then we will figure out what is going on and what to do about it."

Even as I say this, it's already too late to slip out quietly. Tom has returned and he drops two plates of food in front of us. The plates shatter on impact, but that's fine because what he has brought out is inedible. The food, if you want to call it that, is wet

SHAUN MEEKS

and bloody, glimmering blue and yellow under the crimson gore. I know what it is right away and my fears have been solidified.

Before us, on the ruined plates are sliced up Gloudians, served like steak tartar. I remember that the mayor had been getting some of the local restaurants to serve up the alien fare, so obviously Tom's is one of those places. Taking a wild guess, it seems Tom has been sampling the food he's been serving. That would explain his illness and how strange he's acting. Now I have to wonder how many others are having the same reaction.

At the time I found out that people were eating the Gloudians, I didn't give it much thought, other than thinking it disgusting. I've heard that eating the flesh of some species— Gloudians can now be added to that list—can have some terrible side effects. Sometimes it's just bad diarrhea, other times it's death. By the looks of Tom, who is now oozing greenish fluids from his mouth and eyes, eating the meat of a Gloudian causes infection. I wonder how bad it is, how it might affect him. Is it just a form of dementia, causing an inability to function, or is it worse? I wonder this right up until he pulls a knife from his apron and comes at me.

Worse.

"You!" he screams and dives at me.

I push back from the table, knock my chair over and get out of the way as fast as I can. He smashes into the table clumsily and falls to the ground.

"Rouge. Get out of here. Go to the sheriff's car, lock the door and keep low."

I can see she's scared but she is too smart to stick around and ask questions when everything goes nuts. She runs out the door just as Tom gets back up off the floor.

"Tom? What are you doing?" the sheriff asks, but Tom pays him no mind. His eyes are fixed on me.

"I know who you are, hunter. Killer. Murderer. You here to kill me too? Is that it? To kill us all?" He swipes the blade at me, but I'm too far away for him to hit. I circle away from his knife hand, towards the sheriff as he continues, "I see you for what you are. Your lies and your schemes. You think you are better, but we're both in the same boat."

"Tom? You need to put down the knife and calm down. There are kids in here, Tom."

Nothing is getting through to him at this point. He's not Tom anymore. He might as well be a zombie. I get to the sheriff's side, pull his gun and aim it at Tom. The sheriff tries to stop me as I cock the hammer, so I waste no time. I pull the trigger and put a bullet through Tom's head. The bullet smacks him in the left eye and blows out the back, spraying a woman running for the door in his meaty mess. Tom lets out a strange cry, like an amplified mouse squeak, and then hits the ground twitching as blood and green fluid leak out of him.

"What the fuck are you doing?" the sheriff screams at me as he charges, tackling me to the ground. "Are you nuts? You just killed a man! My friend! You're done, asshole."

He tries to flip me over, and I can hear that he's pulled his handcuffs out to arrest me. I struggle, but before I have to fight him too hard, all hell breaks loose for a second time.

Gibson holds me as still as he can as someone screams from the kitchen area. As he looks over, I feel him loosen his grip and his body goes limp. I turn my gaze the way, sure that I'm going to see some other zombie-like person, but I am not prepared for this.

A woman that I can only assume is Tom's wife, stands by the counter, swaying back and forth. She shrieks over and over again as she looks at her dead husband. I'm pretty sure she is oblivious to the fact that the right side of her face is bubbling out and pulsating as though it is ready to blow. Green fluid seeps from a small fissure under her eye and as she takes a step towards us, I push Gibson off me and grab the gun I dropped when he knocked me down.

"We should get out of here now, Sheriff."

There is now other movement in the coffee shop. People are running for the door, but there are a few that are infected and they are trying to follow the ones on the run.

"What the fuck is wrong with Betty?" Gibson screams, looking back and forth from me to Tom's wife.

"They ate some bad fish," I say, wondering just how many people in town did the same.

The old man down at the lake, others down on their luck and struggling to afford food; so many of the town will be in the same boat. This was going to get much worse before it got better.

I've never heard of any way to cure someone that has changed in this way. It's going to be a problem if as many people have eaten the dead Gloudians as I'm calculating. How will the mayor explain why the population in Innisfil has been cut in half?

I push the sheriff towards the door, keeping an eye on Betty as I do. She doesn't seem too interested in us at the moment. Her eyes are on her dead husband. As she leans down to him, the levy that is holding back the flood gates of whatever is in the giant boil on her finally lets go and showers Tom with thick, green pus. I'm trying not to gag, as I keep pushing Gibson towards the door. Some of the infected citizens are almost at the door too. Gibson is out, but some of them block my exit so I have to shoot a woman and a teenage boy in the face. Not my best moment, but there is little else to do. Others scream as red and green mist the air, but I have hurry to follow the sheriff.

Gibson jumps in the car and I follow suit. I look into the backseat and I'm glad to see that Rouge is there, hiding still despite our return. The car moves forward, tires skidding and she looks up at me from the floor.

"What was that all about?" she asks.

"They ate some bad fish."

She gives me a look, one that I have never seen before, and I know right away that it means this is not a time to make jokes. She's right, but sometimes you have to laugh to keep from crying. Cops do it all the time, although I think Gibson isn't pleased that I'm making light of the situation right now.

"Seriously, do you have any idea what the fuck that was?" the sheriff says as he turns down a random street.

I explain that people in town have been bringing the bodies of the dead Gloudians home and tried to eat them. I tell them about the fisherman I saw by the lake and how he thought it was some new type of fish. Rouge thinks this is crazy, and I concur. I tell her that the mayor even went so far as to encourage some of the local restaurants to begin serving the creatures as a way to cut back on costs, which she can't quite believe.

"Who the hell would eat those things? I mean, if they are as nasty as you describe, you'd have to be out of your mind."

"I know people who have. Live next door to some of them in

fact," Gibson says, reminding me that even his neighbor had eaten a Gloudian or two. I can see he's worried, but I push on.

I speculate that what's going on is that the town is infected by the Gloudians and are now turning into zombies. More like the DNA of the Gloudians has gotten into their bloodstream and changed their entire makeup. The people that ate them seem to be hybrids, retaining their own memories and those of the Gloudians they ate, hence how they know who I am. Some people's bodies seem to reject the DNA, like Betty, and erupt with pus and blood until they end up dying.

"So how do we stop it? How can we change them back?" Gibson asks as he drives like a crash derby participant.

"Stop it? Well, you saw how to stop it." I hold up the gun. "This is the only thing that's going to stop them."

"What? We kill everyone that's infected? Jesus Christ man, you have to be kidding me! How many people are we talking here?"

"Who knows how many ate the creatures. This isn't common. People don't normally go around eating dead monsters they find in the lake. The circumstances of anything similar were vastly different, and killing the changed was the only way to contain them."

"Wait," Rouge jumps in from the backseat. "Contain them? As in they can spread this and infect others?"

"It's a possibility. One of the times I know about, a race of monsters that invaded another planet. When they got there, the leader decided that he and his army would eat the flesh of the conquered. They all became infected. They then returned to their planet, close to insane from the change, and infected the rest of their race. That could be what's happening here. But I can't be certain. To know for sure, we'll have to wait to see if someone who didn't eat the creatures changes too."

"I'm so glad I came here to visit you," Rouge says and sits back in her seat.

I feel bad. I was so happy to see her when I opened my motel room door, so glad to have her kissing me and in my bed, that I feel like a jackass putting her here in the middle of it all. I know now that I've been taking the ease of these jobs for granted lately, or else I would never have let her to stay. I'd already known there was a portal situation before she showed up, so why hadn't I put her in that cab and sent her back to the city? One look at her in the rear-view mirror answers that question.

I'm crazy for her.

"I'm sorry I got you into this, Rouge. I should have sent you home."

"Don't blame yourself, Dillon. I'm a big girl and make my own choices. You didn't tell me to bring the bag to you, Godfrey did. But I don't blame him either. I knew what you did, it was my choice. But, I'm just saying, this is the last time I visit you at work."

I smile and turn to Gibson.

"So where exactly are we going?"

"I don't know. Away from there though. Maybe we should head to the station and get some weapons."

Guns will be good, on the infected at least, but there will still be the other Gloudians to deal with. Not to mention the portal. Guns won't work against those things. I need to get my stuff and I need the bag that was stolen from me.

"We should go back to my motel room first. I need to grab my gear before we do anything else."

"The station is right there though," he says and I see it's less than a block away.

"Let's hurry then."

We stop there and luckily there's no infected around. I ask Rouge if she wouldn't mind getting down on the floor again and hiding out until we get back.

"Why aren't I coming with you?" she protests.

"It's safer for you in here. I doubt anything will notice you. And I'll leave you this." I hand her Gibson's gun.

She takes it reluctantly and moves back down to her hiding spot in the footwell.

We step out of the car. Rouge gives one final protest, saying she's never shot a gun outside of a video game, and I lean in quickly to give her the basic instructions.

Point. Shoot.

That should be enough, since we'll get in and out of the station, and then go grab my weapons. There's no time to tell her about squeezing as opposed to pulling the trigger or about the kick a gun has. All I can really do is hope that she doesn't need to use it.

We run inside and the place is empty, which I can tell from Gibson's expression is not a good thing. Gibson stops two feet inside and looks around. I wait to see what he does.

"What is it?" I ask.

"Mary isn't here. It should be her day on. She's our dispatcher," he explains. "Shit. Where is she?"

"Where is who?"

We both jump at the woman's voice behind us. I spin around expecting to see an infected. I have nothing to defend myself, so I reach towards one of the plastic plants, ready to grab it and do what with it...I have no idea. Tickle her?

Luck for us though, she seems normal. As normal as someone can be when wearing a pink track suit covered in the ugly, warped heads of cats. She smiles at us, sips her steaming ugly cat mug, and sits behind her desk.

"You okay, Sheriff? You look a bit pale."

"I'm fine, Mary. Actually, I'm in a bit a rush. Any strange calls today?"

"Only the usual. Preston has been calling, going on and on about how it's urgent he speaks to you. His usual. Something about a conspiracy he's uncovered,; dark, shadowy men in town. No doubt he was watching X-Files again and thinks we are getting attacked by aliens or something, right?" She snort-laughs.

Gibson nods at her before he tells me to follow him.

"And who is this?"

"Sorry. Mary, this is Dillon. Dillon, this is our dispatcher, Mary."

"I'm more than that. I do everything around here really. I'm like a police mom." She holds her hand out for me to shake. I do and she gives me a strange wink. "You two friends?"

"Sort of." Gibson says and we head toward the back rooms. "Let me know if you get anything else out of the ordinary."

"Will do."

We leave Mary to answer the phone that starts ringing as the door is closing behind me.

"She's a weird one. This town seems full of them." I say, but he doesn't respond. "Does she like cats or what?"

"Just one cat. Her dead one. Ugly little thing she called Poncho Pants. Strange damn name for a cat if you ask me. Here we go."

We get to the gun case and he pulls out two pistols, a shotgun and a whole lot of ammo. Everything ends up in a large black bag in the bottom of the case.

"You always keep a big gun bag handy? In case of days like this?" I ask.

"We keep it there so when we head out for target practice we don't come out toting a shotgun and looking like the world is going to end. Same thing now; I'd rather not walk out with shotguns over each shoulder and start a panic."

"Good luck with that." I try to make a joke, but it's getting hard to make light of this at all. "This won't stay quiet for long. Once the infected start getting around, your town is going to get turned upside down. People are going to think it's the end of times. We just have to hope that the situation doesn't get too out of hand before we can start cleaning this mess up."

Gibson doesn't look happy, and I can't blame him. This is his town that's gone to hell. It's got to suck.

"Let's go. We'll get to the motel, grab your gear and then figure out where to go from there."

I'm sure he's just doing his best not to think too much about it all. I do my best to help out, offer a hand on his shoulder and give it a squeeze. There's little I can offer in words that will make him feel better, but at least I can give him the old 'I got ya, bro' shoulder squeeze.

As we make it into the front office, I hear Mary on the phone.

"…not at all. There's nothing like that outside your house. You go ahead and ignore it. It's just kids I bet. But, tell you what, if it goes on much longer, call back and I'll see that the Sheriff swings by…Okay?…Not a problem…I will…Take care." She hangs up, shaking her head at us standing by the door. "Jeannette must be skipping her medication again. She thinks there's a zombie in her back yard. Go figure."

"Who is Jeanette?" I whisper to Gibson.

"Old lady. Lives close to the lake," he tells me. "Mary, if she calls back, let me know ASAP. I may just stop by anyway and see what's going on."

"You're a sweet man, sheriff. I think she just wants some attention, but it's nice that you would do that." She clearly has no idea of what's going on. I hope she can stay ignorant.

We head back outside and all but run to the car. Gibson hands me the bag of guns and I nurse it on my lap. I'd rather have them close by just in case. Useful against the infected; not so good against the creatures that have come out of the lake. He starts the car and Rouge sits up, leaning towards us.

"So far so good. I haven't heard any zombie things or screams. That's good right?"

"Can we not call them zombies?" Gibson asks as he drives towards the motel. "It sounds stupid."

"What would you prefer?" Rouge says with a laugh. "Inter-dimensional hybrids? They look and act like zombies. I know they're not, and you know they're not, but I don't think they know they're not."

"It sounds dumb. But call them what you like."

We sit in silence until we reach the motel. I rush in, alone this time, and run to where my weapons are. Or at least to where they should be.

They're not there. Not my gloves, or my blades. The only things in my bag are a baseball bat that will have no proper effect on a Gloudian—although if I hit one over and over again I'm sure it could do some damage—a green candle I use to cast spells on non-physical beings, and a photo of an actress. That last one's just for me. It doesn't help in any way.

I decide not to take anything with me and run back to the sheriff's car. I slam the door and give him a look that lets him know how grim things are.

"What?" he says, missing the point of the look.

"My stuff is gone. Knives and gloves. First the items I need to close the portal gets stolen; now this."

"Wait. You're not talking about those dirty looking work gloves and the cheap knives you had with you on the beach are you?" Gibson asks.

"Yes! Please tell me you have them."

"No. But I do know where they are. They were in your car when I found you all messed up. They looked like garbage, so I left them there."

I sigh. Someone could have taken them from there too, but I have to find out. We don't have many other options.

"We need to get out to my car and fast."

"Why not just use the guns?" Gibson asks with confusion.

"The guns are fine for anyone that has changed like Tom, but won't work against the monsters coming out of the lake. The only way to kill them is with those knives, burning or drowning them. Though I'm sure if you decapitated one with a shotgun blast, it would do the trick. There's likely to be way too many to deal with that way, and we don't have the shells to do it. The knives will be the surest way; if they're still there."

I can see he still has question, but I doubt he will get it. I could tell him that the flesh of these creatures is not natural to this world, so weapons from here like bullets, stakes, spears or blades will do little to harm them. I'm not even that sure that they'd penetrate through their skin. I'm struggling to explain it in a way he will understand, until I come up with an easy analogy. If he's a comic book fan, this will be easier.

"Think of them like Superman. They are alien to this world and are given powers they might not have elsewhere. That means the only way to kill them is to use a weapon from their world. Like you'd use kryptonite to hurt or kill the Man of Steel. It's the same idea with the Gloudians. Only in this case, it is spellbound knives."

"So the knives are like kryptonite to them?"

"In a manner of speaking," I say and behind me Rouge chuckles. "What?"

"Are all men comic book nerds?" she says and jabs me in the shoulder. "And the idea of you fighting a bunch of Supermen and coming out on top is kind of hot. What do these things look like? Are they as handsome as Clark Kent?"

"No," both Gibson and I say in unison.

"Ugly?"

"Like a blue and yellow baboon's ass," I tell her. "Only with a whole lot of teeth."

"Oh."

I'm sure she's trying to picture just how bad they will be.

Hopefully she won't get to see any of them up close. The rest of the drive to the lake is quiet.

When we get to my car, relief washes over me when I see that the bloody knives and gloves are still in it. I open the door as fast as I can, grab them and turn back to the sheriff's car. As I walk back, both of them look at me through the windshield, pale and frozen. I pause, and know right away that there is something behind me. I almost ask them what it is, but then I hear the terrible clicking and hissing chorus of Gloudians.

A lot of Gloudians.

Well, here comes round two, I think to myself, and slip the gloves on as I spin round. As soon as I turn, I see why they both went so pale. It looks as though the entire horizon has been turned the yellow and blue of their glittering skin. There must be over five hundred of them. I won't stand a chance in this fight.

"Start the car!" I yell as I sprint back to Gibson's police cruiser.

"Gogogogogogogogogo!" I scream in a panic and as he spins the car around to drive away from the beach, I reach over, grab the door and throw myself inside. The door slams hard against my leg and I cry out, but my voice is drowned in the bellowing screams of the Gloudians outside the car.

"Are they as fast as they look?" Rouge asks as she looks through the back window of the car at the approaching swarm.

"They're fast, but let's hope this car is faster." I say and put my hand on Gibson's shoulder. "Is this as fast as your squad car goes?"

"Buckle up," he says as the engine guns and the pressure of the car's speed builds. "I put a Corvette engine in last year. Let's hope I did a good job."

I'm relieved by the distance that grows between us and the Gloudians as the sheriff accelerates. I let out a sigh of relief and hope that they don't follow us back to town. If their purpose is to kill me and prepare for the arrival of the Hellion, then I should assume they'll follow us. And if they do, we need to be ready to kill a large group of them, as fast as we can.

I remember that Hickner said that if I sent him back, Rector the Hellion would provide a new body and send him again and again until the job was done. If that's true, then using the knives won't do enough to stop them.

I need to give them a true death. Every last one of them, which won't be an easy task. We're going to need some sort of trap. Burning them all might be the easiest way to go, but how?

As Gibson drives I try to figure out how I'm going to do this. Since I don't really know this town all that well I am about to ask the sheriff where he thinks might be a good place. Before I can, the car slams to a halt and I hear the man behind the wheel curse under his breath. What now?

I look out the window and see just what it is that has his knickers in a bunch. In front of us, the street is filling up with the infected townspeople. Most of them are stumbling strangely as though they don't know how to use the limbs they were born with. They gyrate and wobble on unsteady legs, and begin to turn towards us.

It's not just their limbs that they don't seem used to. The faces of these poor fools that thought it was a good idea to eat a creature that looked so utterly alien, have taken on characteristics of the Gloudians, and they look grotesque. For some of them, their skin just looks slack on their bones and skulls, punctuated with open sores oozing green fluids. These might be the ones that are rejecting the hybrid DNA, the ones that will die easily on their own. Others look as though they have exploded out of their human skin and now glisten with new green, blue and yellow flesh. Some look partially melted with their bones exposed, seeping red and yellowish pus from gaping wounds.

A woman close to us, that looks like a hybrid, opens her mouth and tries to scream, but all that comes out of her mouth is her tongue. The slab of pink meat falls from between her cracked lips and hits the road, flops for a second before laying still. The tongue's former owner doesn't look at it at all, or even seem concerned. Instead she walks towards us, pointing, bloody mouth still open.

"Jesus. I think that's Shelly McCormick. She lives a few houses away from me. Oh my god, what the fuck is going on?"

"She isn't that person any more, sheriff. She's gone. They all are. If you want to save your town, you need to know that. We need to worry about the normal folk. Not the ones already lost to us."

I unzip the bag and pull out a riot shotgun. We need to clear the road and the only way to do it is to kill them all. It feels terrible, but as far as I can tell, they're all lost to us. I pump the gun, take aim and fire.

Fire.

Fire.

The sheriff and Rouge get out of the car and join in. Luckily the infected are slow, so the job is easier than movies make it out. They don't need head shots to die either, which makes it easier, though I do take out a couple that way. Not proud of it, but it's not every day you get to shoot someone in the head with a shotgun. I'm also a better shot than I thought.

We keep shooting; the street is turning red with blood as the bodies fall. As they come towards us, they are dropped, none able to get closer than ten feet before they're killed. I reload fast, as do the others and worry that we might run out of ammo soon, but after a few minutes it's all done. We're alone on the street, the infected lie motionless in pools of blood and gore. I toss the gun into the car and start walking towards them.

Now comes the worst part.

"What are you doing?" Rouge asks as I open my door.

"We need to clear the road." The guns are gone, but I keep my knives on me, just in case any of them are still holding on to life. "We can't drive over all these bodies. Come on."

I make my way towards the dead that litter the road. Rouge and the sheriff follow, but they keep their guns close.

We try to work as fast as we can to clear the road. The smell coming off the dead is worse than any corpse I have ever smelt before; a combination of rotting meat, B.O. and stale urine. It's from their new DNA. I try not to gag, like the others are, but it's tough not to. I try and decide whether I would rather smell them or taste them and choose to breathe through my nose in the long run. Better not to have the infected in my mouth.

At one point I look over at the sheriff and Rouge as the two of them pull a body toward the roadside. Rouge is having a hard time, she's probably has never seen death like this before, but when I look at the sheriff, he is taking it much worse. He's near tears as he drags a corpse across the street and lets it go on the soft shoulder. I walk over to him before he gets another body.

"You okay?" I ask.

"No. I'm not okay at all. I knew these people; some were friends of mine. Jesus! I had dinner with that guy over there last week. His name's Bob. We've know each other since grade school, and now he's dead. This is not how the world is supposed to work."

"You have no idea how insane the world really is, Hank." I put my hand on his shoulder.

I think about telling him a story of some other craziness I've dealt with once before, like the kid with the demon-possessed mullet, but before I can, the hot punch of an explosion knocks us all to the ground.

I hit the concrete hard. When I look back toward the source, I see the sheriff's car engulfed in flames. Around the ruins are more infected, a group of Gloudians congregating near them. I quickly get to my feet, help the sheriff up and then run over to Rouge who is struggling to stand. Both of them are fine, but if we don't get out of there, they won't be that way for long.

"What was that?" she asks as she gets to her feet. She goes to turn but I pull her towards the sheriff and the woods.

"No time for that. We need to get out of here now."

There's only one way to go. I look past the sheriff, to the woods behind him, and know that it's the only chance we have. My stomach quivers at the sight of them. Dark trees loom before us, inviting us into the darkness; the darkness and the bugs. I shudder. I wish there was some other way, but since there isn't, I know I have to just suck it up and run for my life.

We run through the woods and I wonder how many bullets each of them have. It's clearly not enough to stand our ground for very long. I yell at them both to save their bullets and run. I take the lead, but have no idea where I am leading them. I only want to put as much distance between the group that blew up the car and us.

The sheriff suggests we stop for a moment so that he can get his bearings, but we can't risk it. He says okay, probably figuring I mean that the townsfolk will catch up to us, which is better than him knowing that I'm more afraid of spiders than of the infected and monsters.

We run for a long time. I can hear unearthly cries in all directions. I try not to think about where we are going, because if I do, I may start to consider that we are heading into a trap. That is a worry; that somewhere in here there is a going to be a large group, waiting to jump us. I don't want to think about this, but looks like I can't help it.

Then we finally break through the trees, safe and sound, but I have no idea where we are. It's a small, tree-lined street with some expensive-looking houses. I ask the sheriff where we are.

"Close to Main Street. If we head west here, we'll get to Branson Road and that'll take us straight there. Is that where you want to go?"

"City Hall may be the safest place for us right now. The place is built like a fortress." It's the only thing that makes sense to me at this point. With the heavy doors and barred windows, it could be our best bet for surviving.

We head along the street, keep an eye out for anything

creepy. Rouge is as close to me as she can be without physically attaching her body to mine. I don't mind. It's nice to feel her warmth and I just hope that we can get out of this in one piece. She gives me a forced smile. I reach out and touch her hand.

"It'll be fine," I whisper.

We're about to turn onto the road that'll lead us to Main Street, but the road is packed with the infected. With the minimal ammo we have and the amount of them there, we won't be able to clear the road; it would appear that it's a lost cause.

"Shit." Rouge whispers, trying not to be noticed by them. We pull back a little, letting the cover of a fence hide us. "Now what?"

"No idea." I tell her honestly and turn to ask the sheriff if he has any ideas, when I see someone waving at us from a backyard. I squint to try to see who it is, but I can't tell. Rouge and the sheriff quickly notice him too.

"Preston?"

Ah! That's why he looks familiar. The security guard that thinks he's a cop. He waves us over anxiously and we hurry to him, pushing through some bushes to get there. He is geared up. He looks like an Emergency Task Force guy in his tactical gear. He's loaded up with guns; there are three hand guns in different holsters in his over-sized bulletproof vest and he has a shotgun strapped to his back and an AK-47 in his hands. This guy has been clearly been expecting an apocalyptic event for a while.

"Jesus, Preston. What the hell are you doing with all these guns?" the sheriff asks. "Does your mom know about them all?"

"She sure does. I knew a day like this was coming. Zombies! I told the guys online that it was going to happen, but they all thought I watched too many movies. Now look at this place. Real, motherfucking zombies all over the place. I told you the other day I had been seeing weird shit. I had info for you, and you didn't give me the time of day. Now look at what we're facing. The goddamn apocalypse."

Preston talks the way a nerd thinks a tough guy should. He keeps his mouth almost completely shut and his teeth gritted, trying his best to look like Dirty Harry, but comes off like a guy with his mouth wired shut. Still, he has guns and may be able to help us fight off some of the infected.

"Do you have any more guns?" Rouge asks before I can do it myself.

"Does a bear shit in the woods? Follow me."

We move behind him, hopping from one backyard to the next, until we get to his house. Just looking at the small house with three Canadian Flags posted in the backyard, tells me so much about him. There is pride in the country you live in and then there's zealous nationalism. I wonder if the inside is going to be as bad, but I never find out. Instead, Preston leads us over to a tool shed that turns out to be a bomb shelter. I had no idea people still built these and they weren't out of old movies and episodes of the Twilight Zone.

"Go down the stairs," he tells us as he locks the door. "The light is on the left hand side."

Rouge is the first in and she hits the switch, flooding the dark room with light. I hear her chuckle right away.

"You have got to be kidding me," she says and when I get into the small, cramped room, I see why.

The place is about ten feet in every direction. There is a stainless steel toilet in one corner, one wall is dedicated to canned food and bottles of water, while the other two walls house nothing but guns and knives of all sizes. I look at them all. Pistols, shotguns, machine guns and rocket launchers beside swords, machetes and daggers. On a small table there's riot helmets and two other bulletproof vests. Preston must have been expecting an all-out war.

He comes down, smiles as he sees that we're all in awe of his insane collection of weapons, and then sits on the closed toilet. There's nowhere for the rest of us to sit now so we stand there looking at the arsenal.

"So, you think this will help you at all?" he asks.

"I would say so," I reply.

"Too bad this place isn't a bit bigger, or I would just suggest we stay here," the sheriff says.

"No kidding. But there is no way I want to do my business in front of the three of you. Spoils my lady-like illusion if I have to drop a deuce," Rouge laughs and we all laugh at that. I'm not sure the laughs are because what she says is funny and slightly ridiculous, or if it's due to the stress.

I walk over to the wall of food and pick up a tin of fruit cocktail. Not something I would normally choose to eat, but it seems better than beans, which is the only other option. I'm starving. I down the first can and as I start a second, I see that everyone else has the same idea. We all eat between four and six of the small tins of syrupy goodness, and then it's time to get back to business.

"So, do you three have any clue as to what is going on?" Preston asks.

"I'll give you the CliffsNotes," I start. "There's a portal under the lake opened by a demon known as a Hellion. He opened the portal using a being called a Porter, which acts as a gateway between two worlds. He's been sending his slaves, a race of creatures called Gloudians, here in order to get my attention and so they can kill me. For some reason it's only when I'm dead that Rector will step into this world. But many of the Gloudians died or committed suicide when they came through and it seems as though a lot of people in your town thought it would be just fine to eat them, despite what they look like. Those that were hungry or stupid enough to eat them became infected. Some turned into a hybrid Gloudian; others haven't been so lucky and it seems like they're slowly coming apart. I don't know how long it will take them to die. They still think like the other hybrids, which means that want me dead. I'm also not sure how contagious they are.

"Now we want to get to City Hall, where I hope the mayor might still be if he hasn't become infected too, and call in the National Guard or whatever we can to help us take care of the infected so that I can go to the lake and close the gate. After I find my bag of course."

"Wow. That's some kind of story." Preston tosses an empty tin on the floor and turns to the sheriff. "I was trying to tell you there was something weird going on when I saw you yesterday and today too. I've been seeing weird stuff for over a week now."

"Like what?" I ask.

"There have been strange people around town. Like those men in black, only these guys weren't in black suits. Actually, I couldn't tell you how they were really dressed. They seemed more like shadows of people than real people. I've seen them around Main Street and down by the lake and with some of the townspeople. And I don't mean just talking to them, but going into their houses. People that normally hate out-of-towners have been taking in strangers. Some of them were even going into city hall. Probably trying to act inconspicuous, right?"

"I guess." I'm not making any sense of what he's saying. The Gloudians aren't shape shifters and I haven't seen anything other than them in town so far. What he's describing sounds familiar though, yet I'm not sure how it relates. Looking around the room though, I have to wonder if it's Preston being paranoid. "But whatever they are, I need to get my stolen bag and then get to the lake. To do that, we need to use some of these guns and get out there. It's time to put an end to it all and set your town straight again."

"I agree." The sheriff walks over to the wall of guns. He looks like a kid in a candy store. "You have ammo for all these?"

"Yep. They're all ready and loaded. Take your pick."

And we all do. Rouge and Gibson put their nearly empty guns down and walk over to the wall. I grab what I'm told is a Tech 9, Rouge takes two Glocks and the sheriff takes one of the AK-47s. The gun I have is lighter than I would have expected, but maybe that's why it's a favorite of street gangs. Preston takes his own guns, two monsters that look more like grenade launchers than actual guns and then loads up a gym bag with spare clips for all of us.

"Let's go cut us down some motherfuckers!" Preston yells and runs back up the stairs, back into the daylight.

We all follow, but I'm feeling a little less enthusiastic than he is. I just want to get it all over with and head home to relax. Being too anxious or excited for a job can easily lead to a slip up, and there's no room for errors right now.

Usually my cases take less than a day and are less work than this is proving to be. It's not often that I have an entourage or a gun in my hand. I'm feeling a bit out of my league with all of this. When I get to City Hall, I'm going to tell the mayor that he owes me a hell of a lot more money than he originally offered. This is too much like real work.

When I get out of the house and into the backyard, I expect to see the place swarming with crazed townies, but there's nothing. I let out a sigh of relief and follow the sheriff as he leads us through backyards towards City Hall. Preston protests quietly. He thinks it would be better to go out in the street and be a movie hero. It takes a bit of work for us to convince him that it's a dumb idea. The heroes in movies like to run out like cowboys and save the day and get the girl, but in reality, the hero would be the first to die. So, although he wants to show us that he could beat Clint Eastwood and Bruce Willis in a dick-swinging contest, Preston stays with us as we keep hidden and safe.

"I bet you're glad you came to see me," I whisper to Rouge and smile. I'm glad to see her smile back at me, looking pretty hot as she crouch runs with two guns in her hands.

"What's life without a little adventure, right? And I'll appreciate it all the more when I get back to my house in one piece, able to remember this instead of living it. I'm sure my puppy will be happy to see me whole again."

"Sorry about this. I owe you big time."

"Is that a promise?"

She smiles and my cheeks burn.

I hope that the situation doesn't get too much worse than it already is. I'd really like to see where things go with Rogue. If I get her killed or maimed, that'll really hurt my chances. She seems pretty cool with how messed up it is right now, but that might change if she goes home missing a body part.

The sheriff stops.

"What is it?" I ask.

"There's City Hall." He points through the trees. "If we're going to get to it, we need to break cover. There's no way around it."

"What's it look like out there?" I ask.

"There are a few of those messed up people," he says.

"You mean zombies, Sheriff? Why can't you just say what they are?" Preston says angrily.

"Shut up, Preston. They aren't fucking zombies. Not exactly." The sheriff shoots Preston a hard look and the wannabe cop backs down. "I hope you have a plan, Dillon?"

"A plan?" I say nervously. "Well, not exactly. I was hoping you'd have a good idea of how to get there without being seen. Like maybe a secret tunnel that runs under the place?"

"There's no good way to get there. This isn't some big city where they might need passages like that. We're going to have to run out into the street and take things as they come."

"At least we have these." Rouge holds up her guns. "We might have to just blast anyone that tries to attack us."

"I don't like that idea," Gibson says as he looks out at the street. "These people voted me in as sheriff. Now I'm supposed to kill them? Jesus! Are we sure what's happened to them is irreversible?"

"Like I said," I remind him, "nothing is certain. I've never seen this happen before. There's no recovering from what I was told. Once they've been infected by the blood or flesh of a Gloudian, I don't think there's any going back. Sorry, Hank."

"Then I say fuck it! We go for it and do what we got to do." Preston suddenly breaks cover before anyone can stop him. He turns to see if we're going to follow his lead.

"Oh hell!" Gibson groans and then follows him. I do too and Rouge brings up the rear.

As soon as we are all out in the open, I hear screams to my left. Three of the infected come towards us, moving faster than the others were earlier. I wonder if they're getting used to their changed forms.

"Oh shit!" Rouge gasps as she sees them too.

We're about fifty yards from the doors of City Hall, so there's no way we can just run for them. They'll either cut us off or see exactly where we went. Then we'll be surrounded by infected and Gloudians trying to get in. As secure as the building might be— and I'm not even sure how secure it is—it might not hold up to the force of all of them. We're going to have to take a stand here and cut as many down until we can get into City Hall unseen.

I raise the Tech 9 and take a deep breath. I've never really shot a gun like this before, but I've read books about them and try to remember what they say.

Deep breath.

Squeeze the trigger, don't pull it.

No more than a three round burst and get ready for the recoil.

So, I do take the steps and squeeze the trigger. I expect thunder to explode from the gun and the feeling of a jackhammer in my hand. But that's not what happens.

The gun makes a weak, almost pathetic mechanical sound, more like an electric toothbrush, followed by a FOOP FOOP FOOP sound. I am confused and stop firing; the infected in front of us keep coming unfazed. And I'm not surprised. What I shot at them is about as deadly as spitballs.

"What the fuck, Preston? Are these Airsoft guns?" Gibson booms and when I turn I see he's dropped his gun and has grabbed Preston by the front of his shirt.

"Yeah, so?"

"So? What the hell are Airsoft guns going to do? Why didn't you tell us they weren't real guns?" Gibson booms and looks like he's going to kill Preston.

"Airsoft?" Rouge and I ask at the same time, as the infected move closer.

"BB guns. Fancy toys for stupid people and nerds that only wish they had real guns. Shit!" He pushes Preston backwards and looks in the same direction I just did. "We better run before…"

But it's already too late because the street is being filled with the infected from nearly every direction; maybe twenty in all. Gibson is the first to run and I grab Rouge's hand and follow. I don't bother to look at Preston, who I would love to slug right at the moment, and we hightail it to City Hall. When we get a few feet from the side of the building, I hear a terrible scream and turn in time to see Preston being swarmed by infected. I can barely make out what they're doing, but when I see the dark pool of blood growing at his feet, I know that there's not much hope for him. They last thing I see is his severed head moving above the crowd like a beach ball at a baseball game. I know I should feel bad, but I can't help to think he died like the movie hero he wanted to be.

And he did buy us enough time to get into the building and slam the door shut. Of course I don't think these doors will hold up too long to the crowd out there, but maybe we'll have enough time to barricade them.

I doubt it, but sometimes you just have to have a little hope.

"We should head upstairs to the Mayor's office." Gibson says.

I agree, but ask him to give Rouge and me a second. He heads towards the stairwell to ensure it's clear and waits.

"Listen," I say to Rouge quietly. "I don't want to put you in harm's way anymore. I don't want you to get hurt."

"What do you suggest? At this point I'm up for almost anything."

"Go in there." I point to the women's bathroom. "Hide in there for now. Go in, lock the door if you can, and hide in a stall. Hopefully we can get this done fast and then I will come back for you."

"And if you don't? What if you get killed?" She sounds more than a little concerned.

I reach out and take her hand. She squeezes it and I return it. I wish I could give her a bit of peace of mind, but I don't want to lie. We're facing some pretty bad odds. There's doesn't seem to be a way out of here, there's a whole lot of infected and Gloudians out there, and the Hellion to think about.

"That's not really an option. Dying is not something I'm good at. You just have to trust me."

She looks at me, and then the bathroom, weighing her options.

"I'm not some helpless dame. I did help save your ass earlier. Maybe I should just stay with you."

"I know you did. Believe me, I do. And I owe you for that. But I don't want you to get hurt in any way. This is my job, not yours. Or the sheriff's. After this, I'm leaving him too. So please, do this for me."

"Fine. But I'm not waiting here forever, so you better hurry up."

"I'll do the best I can." I say and before I can walk away, she grabs me and kisses me hard on the mouth, making my head whirl.

"Do better than your best," she says as she disappears into the bathroom. I leave when I hear the door lock.

"Let's go."

The sheriff leads me up the stairs to the mayor's office. As we get to the top, we hear banging on the front and side doors of the building.

"Let's make this as quick as we can," I say as we walk into the mayor's office.

I'm a little surprised to see Fent behind his desk. He's just as calm as can be, smoking a cigar and leaning in his chair. He barely looks at us as we shut the door and Gibson locks it. I get the feeling he's been expecting us.

"What are you doing in here, Fent? Do you have any idea what is going on out there?" Gibson asks and I'm pretty sure he is as confused as I am.

"Why do I care what's going on out there, Sheriff? That's

your job, isn't it? You should be out there, keeping the peace and what not." He sits up and looks from Gibson to me. "And what about you, Dillon? Shouldn't you be out there too, getting rid of all the bad things that have come to town? Isn't that why you were hired?"

He smiles at me and is sweating a lot. But there's something off about him. I half expect to see him change like the others, to become one of the infected, but he looks like he did yesterday.

Sort of.

There's something not quite right with him, but I've no idea what it could be.

"Well, what are you two doing here? Come now, Sheriff; there are monsters outside. And hunter, there's something in the lake, yet you're here. Shouldn't you be there using those knives of yours on the monsters and stopping all of this madness?" He laughs then and lets out a long, smelly belch.

"What the hell is going on here?" This is not the man I saw yesterday, not the man I talked to on the phone. He seems more confident, sure of himself. There's something rotten here.

"I have no idea what you mean. You're the monster detective, shouldn't you have an idea of what's going on? Aren't you the expert?" He laughs and puts his cigar out on the bare desk. "I hired you to come here and find the problem, to get rid of it, so why exactly are you here in my office instead of being out by the lake dealing with the portal?"

Bingo!

"What portal, mayor?" I ask. He shouldn't have any idea what a portal is, shouldn't know that there is a porter somewhere under the lake, yet he mentions one.

"Oops. Guess I shouldn't have said that, right?" Fent laughs and then snaps his fingers.

When he does this, the door to the office crashes open and five infected stumble in with three Gloudians. The group grabs hold of me and Gibson and my heart sinks. I struggle, but there is too many of them to fight. The blades in my belt are removed and as Fent laughs I stop fighting and wait for what is to come. I've been in dicey situations before, but this does not look good for me, or Gibson.

"What now?" I ask, though I'm not sure I want to hear. "Are you going to let your zombies here kill us? Or are you going to let these little shits have their way?"

"Zombies? They're not zombies, Dillon. I know you know that. They are changing, for the better maybe. Soon they will look more like these other little fellas, except they will be my slaves. I have a deal with a certain admirer of yours. He made a bargain with me that I couldn't refuse. All I had to do was bring you here and have you killed on the beach where he could see it from the other side. Then, when he crosses over, I get the town and an army of slaves to do whatever I want with. It's a good deal since I'm pretty sure he plans on wiping out most of the human race. Or at least killing those that he doesn't enslave."

"That is the lamest thing I've ever heard." I laugh and see that Gibson is terrified. I have to try and buy some time while I figure out what to do. I need to keep Fent talking. "You sound like some retarded movie villain that actually believes the lies told to him by a bigger, more powerful villain. That Hellion, he's going to run over you when he gets here. He'll either kill you or make a slave out of you too. You're not safe from him. Nothing here is.

He's a demon, more powerful than you could ever know."

"I disagree, Dillon. I know a lot more right now than you give me credit for. I know what I'll get, as long as I give you up to him. We're wasting time here. We need to get you to the beach where he can see you die." Fent pats my cheek. "It's a shame. There are things I would have liked to experience, but it'll be better in the long run. Well, better for me. I'm looking forward to seeing how this all ends."

"And what about me, Fent?" Gibson yells and he struggles against his captors. "You think I'm going to let you get away with this? You think I'm not someone to be reckoned with?"

"Not really. You're in no state to do anything against me."

Gibson looks as though he's about to ask Fent what he means by that, but before he can, the mayor takes one of my knives from the Gloudian and jams it into the sheriff's left eye. Goo and blood drool down the man's face as Fent twists and turns the blade in the eye socket, stirring the man's brains as he does. Gibson's mouth opens and shuts as though he is trying to say something, but all that comes out is a weird gasp and a wheezing sound. Fent then grabs the other blade and buries it in the man's neck, sawing away until the sheriff's body tears away from his head and hits the floor. Fent pulls the knife free from the ruined eye and tosses the severed head across the room. He walks over to me, wiping the knives off on the front of my shirt.

I want so much to kill this man right now. Not fast like what he just did to Gibson. Some way slow and painful.

"Now," Fent says and turns to the infected holding me, handing my blades back to one of them. "Let's get him down to the beach and be done with all this mess. Our new master is waiting."

A few years ago, I was hired by a couple to come to their house and find what was scratching their child's arms. Their daughter, Samantha was just three years old, but every night she would go to bed and in the morning would wake with terrible red welts on her arms, legs and stomach. Sometimes they were deeper. The parents suspected that the girl had somehow been scratching herself, so they set up a video camera in the room to see for themselves.

In a few days, they went to wake Samantha and found the same cuts. They also found the video camera on the floor, completely smashed. They watched what they could of the video. One second their daughter was in her bed, peaceful as can be; the next minute, the camera was tumbling through the darkness and stopped. They thought it was a ghost and contacted their church, wanting the house exorcized. The priest declined, and then referred them to me, saying that I could help them.

I watched the video and though all they saw was the camera fall, I caught something that they missed. It was no wonder they didn't see it. Unless you were looking for something more, you wouldn't have noticed it at all.

Luckily, I did.

I saw the carpet move a split second before the camera fell. It was a subtle movement, but enough of one that I was sure that the culprit had taken up living in the rug. I sent the family away and went in with a bag of tools. That the daughter was being scratched lead me to believe that it could be a Daaf, a race that known drink the blood of humans, but there was no proof. I went into the situation a little blind. But I did bring a few extra items with me, just in case I was off. There are other species of monsters and demons that would do the same, though most of them wouldn't live in a carpet.

Armed with my tools I went into the room, locked the door and window and turned to the rug.

"So, do you want to show yourself now, or should I just send you back?" I asked.

When there was no response, I walked over to the carpet and pulled out a Teed from my pocket, which is a small bronze coin that looks as though it has a maggot pressed into it. I flipped the Teed in my hand and waited, knowing that if it was a Daaf and it saw the coin it would know I meant business.

Still nothing.

"Well then, I guess this is what you want." I took the coin and pressed it to the carpet, expecting a scream of terrible pain. If a Teed touches a Daaf, it would react the same way as if a human were shot in the stomach with a gun. Yet this one didn't react.

I slid on my gloves and decided then to make the being reveal itself, whatever it was. Before the first one was on though, the carpet moved, slid away from me and took on an almost human-like form, but with a larger head and squat legs. The shape made me certain that it was a Gargar; a weaker race, normally timid, that never use violence.

"Please, don't hurt me," it said as it moved away from me. "I never hurt, Sammy. She's my friend."

Its voice was soft and I could hear its fear. I could also tell by the dialect that it was a Gargar.

"Really? So where did all the scratches come from? Do you normally cut up your friends?"

"No. I would never hurt her. She's just a baby. It's just..." The thing trailed off and looked around the room. "I'm not the only being here. A few things have come and gone since Sammy was born. There are several weak spots here that lead to many different worlds. Most come and go, especially when they see that I already live here. But others, they want to stay. They want to hurt Sammy."

"What wants to hurt her?"

"I...it's not me. It's...him."

"Who's him?" I asked, trying not to lose my patience.

"I better not say. He's not very nice, you know."

I looked around the room, trying to see if there was anything else there with us, but all I saw were toys, the girl's bed and a closet full of baby clothes. I wasn't sure if the Gargar was telling the truth, but I couldn't see why it would lie.

"So, I'm assuming that this other one, the one that's cutting Sammy is a Daaf?" I asked and began to move around the room, pulling the Teed back out of my pocket as I did.

"I can't say yes, but I can't say no either."

"Good enough."

I took the coin and began to touch random things in the room with it, sure that when I got to where the Daaf was hiding, I would know by the screams. I also kept an eye on the Gargar, watched its reaction as I moved towards items and gauged whether I was hot or cold. As I got to the bed that Sammy slept in, I could tell the Gargar was nervous, saw it curl up a little, and knew that the Daaf was near or on the bed. I wondered if it had used the bed itself, or the sheets, or maybe had formed a body using the foam in the mattress.

As it turned out, it was none of them.

I lowered the coin to the bed, ready to touch the sheets, and as I did, something wrapped around my ankle. I let out a little gasp as the grip tightened and then I was pulled off balance. I crashed to the floor, dropping the Teed before I was pulled under the bed. It was dark there, and smelled of hot, garlic breath. I was almost amused that the Daaf had been under the bed, a monster following the most stereotypical of ideas, but as I had no idea what the creature was going to do and because I had dropped my weapon, the humour bled out of me.

I struggled against the creature and managed to get a glimpse as I did. Right away I could tell that he was a Daaf, as his body was long and thin, head narrow and pointed at each end. From what I could tell, he used the dust and dust bunnies from under the bed to call forth a physical form here, something that would probably terrify a kid.

He growled and shrieked at me as I tried to kick his hand off my ankle. His slashed at me with his free hand and I felt the burn of my skin opening. I continued to kick and went to pull out my gloves, but found that I had dropped them too.

It seemed hopeless. My hands would do little to destroy the Daaf.

But then, the coin wheeled beside me. The Gargar, the one that had told me that Sammy was his friend had picked it up and rolled it to me. I quickly grabbed it and pressed it onto the dusty face of the monster. He screamed terribly and let me go, but I didn't let him off so easily. I touched him all over with the Teed and his screams continued until the dust finally fell free and he was no more. The dust was just dust and the monster was sent back to where it should have been all along.

When I was done, I got out from under the bed, dusted myself off and looked at the Gargar quivering in the corner. It knew what I was there to do, knew that it had to be sent back. There are rules, and I was there to enforce those rules.

Still, the scared creature had saved my life, and it really was harmless, so what was I to do in that moment? I had never been one for mercy.

"You know you aren't allowed here, right?" I asked it.

"I know, but Sammy is my friend. I would have protected her if I could, but I thought if I damaged their camera, and I was seen on it, that a hunter would be sent and that filthy, mean bastard would be sent away from her. I only wanted to protect my friend."

"That's all well and good, but…"

"But you have a job. I know. You do what you have to do, just promise me that you'll protect Sammy. Please."

I thought about what it said. Normally, all these beings that crossover do is try and save their own ass. They come here to find out why earth is forbidden, thinking it's better than where they live. Some even come because they are too scared and pathetic to stay where they belong. Yet here was one of them that didn't care if they got sent back, or even died; it just wanted to make sure the little girl was kept safe.

And it saved me, the person sent to dispatch it, to let me help.

"You know what?" I tucked the coin in my pocket. "I think you'd be better suited to protect Sammy, at least for now. You make sure she stays safe and if anything comes to hurt her, you are to find a way to get a hold of me. Deal?"

"You mean I can stay with her?"

"Only if you keep her safe."

"I will. I will make sure nothing ever harms her. Thank you."
I could hear the love in its voice, the gratitude, and its happiness
that for the first time ever, I showed mercy.

There's been moments when I was sure I would be seriously
hurt, maybe even killed, like that time under that bed. I had been
so unarmed, so unable to defend myself and was lucky to have
someone save my ass.

I don't think I'm going to be so lucky this time around.

Nobody is going to rescue me from the infected and the
Gloudians walking me along the streets of Innisfil towards my
demise. More and more of them join us as we go along, and as the
group continues to swell, my hopes shrink.

I know Rouge is still alive, or at least hope she is, but she's
locked in the bathroom. She has no idea that I'm being led to the
lake to be sacrificed so that a Hellion can enter this world.

I still don't fully get why it needs me dead before it can
crossover. Or the reason it's afraid of me. A damn Hellion, afraid
of me.

My thoughts go back to Rouge and I know that if I don't get
out of this bind, she'll be hurt or killed. Hell, the whole world will
fall, but in the end, what do I really care about them. I have no
real ties to anyone alive, aside from Rouge, who I care about with
all my heart. It seems irrational, after knowing her for such a short
time, but I care more about her safety than I do my own. As bleak
as things look right now, I'll fight until my last drop of blood if it
means I have a chance at saving her.

I'm pushed hard from behind as I slow down thinking about
Rouge.

As we move through the streets, I look into the houses we pass, as though I will find some sort of salvation in one of them. People hide behind curtains in a few, no doubt terrified by what they see. It's not every day you get to wake up to see everything you thought right and normal get flipped upside down. The townspeople here lived quiet lives, as close to rural living as you can get without the manual labour. They moved to the middle of nowhere, to an idyllic town to live simply in.

But it seems there isn't really a safe place. Now they're seeing it too. That beneath every blooming flower, there's a shadowy spot, a dark place where beings live who can hurt them. They're probably watching me get dragged down the street by monsters and their own infected friends, maybe even their families, and wonder when their time will come. Soon enough I think, if this Hellion has his way. If I can't put a stop to it all, they're all looking down the same hall of death that I'm looking at right now.

I have to think!

We pass an intersection and I watch as a man is pulled from his truck by two of the further gone infected. Although they still have the height of a human, they've become gaunt with skin all blue and yellow like a Gloudian. The man cries out for help, but no one will come for him. I certainly can't do anything when I should be calling out myself.

The two infected pry the man's mouth open and one vomits greenish liquid into his mouth. I turn away and see how close the beach is. I feel sick at the sight of the water and the whirlpool. My end is nigh.

I need to think, and think fast.

I look down at one of the Gloudians closest to me. He looks just like Hickner. Actually, they all look like him. There's not much to tell one from the other. I wonder if they're bred that way; made to look so much like the next so that when they are sold off there is no call for a more handsome, fit or more beautiful Gloudian. Perfection in the mundane. I feel a bit bad for them.

And maybe that can help.

"Aren't you sick of this? Sick of being a slave to whoever comes along with more power and more money?" I ask the one closest to me.

"Shut up, dead man," it hisses and doesn't even look at me.

"I helped one of your kind, a Gloudian named Hickner. He was tired of being a slave to the highest bidder, to the Hellion that has owned him and used him. He begged for a release from it, a true death so he could be freed from slavery, but maybe he should have done more. Maybe instead of bowing out and letting his life end, he should have stood up and fought to be alive and free. I mean, what good is freedom if you're dead?"

"I said shut up, you piece of shit!"

"Why should I?" I say, talking louder so that more of the Gloudians can hear me. There are hundreds on the beach and I hope that they can me hear too, because if I do this right, it may be my ticket out of this mess. "Why should you live under the thumb of a Hellion or another other being? Where does it say that the Gloudians must be slaves, that they can never determine their own future? Nowhere. You are living creatures with your own destiny. You shouldn't be owned. You need to see that and stand up to take what is yours: your freedom.

"There was once slavery on this planet too. Races of people

held down and sold off as though they were property. But they fought back, and when they did, others joined their fight. Races stood together to stand against the aggressors until one day they were free. Free! You should all be able to taste the air as free creatures, just as they did."

"How about I rip your tongue out of your mouth?" one of the infected slurs with his warped speech. I ignore him. Many of the Gloudians are listening to me, some of them even nodded.

"Why don't you keep quiet, newbie. Damn half-breed!" One of the Gloudians barked at the infected one that had spoken up. "You have no idea what we've been put through."

There was mumbling from the other Gloudians and I could see many of them were now watching me, listening. I had to keep it going.

"I spoke to Hickner and he told me how terrible life is for your kind. It's not right that I have to send any of you back, especially when it's to a place where you are slaves, where you have nothing. You are living, sentient beings. Your kind deserves to be free. Freedom isn't a privilege; it's a right."

There are cheers among the Gloudians and I could see those who weren't agreeing are being convinced by others. There were nods and applause and then I noticed we were no longer moving forward. The beach was only twenty feet away, but we had stopped. I felt like Braveheart, or like Maximus from Gladiator, but if I could sway them, maybe I could get out of this in one piece.

I'm about to speak again when I am pushed hard from behind by one of the infected and I nearly fall forward. I fight to stay upright as a wave of screams erupts around me. For a second my heart stops. I think that they're all about to attack and kill me, despite my speech. But as the screaming continues and I'm not hit, cut or stabbed, I realise it might be something else. It's more like battle cries.

I look back to see six of the Gloudian have jumped on the infected that pushed me. He tries to fight them off, but they are biting and tearing at him with their sharp claws and teeth. Dark green blood spills from his mouth and he falls to his knees, holding ropes of intestines that have been torn from him. His eyes meet mine and for a moment, everything is quiet; the infected and the Gloudians watch as he sways back and forth.

Then, as he slumps and his face slams into the ground, an all-out war breaks out. Gloudians and the infected are fighting, ripping at each other. I back away, not wanting to get in the middle of the fray and I'm smacked in the face with a severed head. I cry out and run down the beach. I hide behind an overturned rowboat while the fighting ensues. I'm not a coward, but I'd rather be an observer than worry about getting injured. Better to wait until the numbers dwindle before I do anything else.

The viciousness of the Gloudians has caught the infected off guard. The infected hybrids just can't keep up with the creatures that were born monsters. The infected really do move too much like zombies to put up much of a fight, but they give it their all. I see some of the Gloudians drop to the ground, mortally wounded, but more of the infected fall than they do.

In my excitement and awe, I've forgotten that I need to get out of here. There's still the Porter beneath the whirlpool and an open door where a Hellion is standing, waiting to come through.

Still, without my bag there's not a whole hell of a lot that I can do to stop it. I want to move, but there's not many places I can run. The entire horizon is a battle scene and at my back are the lake and whirlpool. I have no other choice but to wait it out. I do hope that when it's all over, the Gloudians are still on my side and don't try to kill me. I hope they'll let go of their grudge.

How many will be left, or at least how many of them will still be in shape to fight at the end of this? Sure, I don't have any weapons, but I have a job to do, and if I'm lucky I will be able to find my gloves and knives before I have to handle them.

It would be easier for me to just get the hell out of dodge. Safer, sure, but then what? They'll have to be dealt with sooner or later. Better now, when they're weak and tired. And even though the odds might still be in their favour, it's a risk I have to take. Even with weapons, it'd be something like two hundred to one. If I was a betting man, I'd give the odds to them.

One of the infected has spotted me. He only has one arm left intact and is spilling blood and milky green goo from where the other used to be. There's also a deep gash in his chest, but he doesn't seem bothered by it as he charges my way. He screams, stumbles and continues in my direction. As I stand, I spot a piece of driftwood close to my foot. It's not the best weapon for defense, but it's better than nothing. The wood is still wet and feels a bit spongy to me. I have a feeling it's not going to do anything. I pick it up, turning quickly back towards the infected townie. When he's close enough, I swing it and connect with his head.

Most of the wood shatters on impact, but what's left is close to a stake. I recover fast and swing again, only this time it's more of stabbing motion. The tip of the dark wood slides into the infected man's neck easily. Dark blood sprays from the wound and the creature stumbles backwards, grasping at the wood as he does. He cries out like a dying cat, until finally his hand grabs the protrusion and yanks it free. That only seems to make it worse. Blood bubbles out of the wound, green and foamy, and his hand tries to apply pressure no doubt, but it's too late. The wound is fatal and he falls to the ground.

Now I'm weaponless again. Damn it.

I look back towards the battle, but it seems like it's already over. The remaining Gloudians stand there, stained in the blood of the infected, but alive. Some are injured, while others are on the ground, dying or dead. But they won and I know that this is big for them.

They are a race of slaves, born to be used, to serve, but they have fought not for someone else, but themselves. It's their first taste of freedom. I have to hope they are feeling like I had a hand in it and don't attack me.

"Dillon; famous monster hunter!" one barks out and moves forward. I wonder if he is the same one that took charge earlier and egged the others on as I first started to talk. "Are you going to send us all back to where we came from now? Back to the Hellion?"

I shake my head. "Even if I had my knives or my tools, I think we proved a point here today."

As the others pause and watch, I'm hoping they don't turn me into a scratching post.

"Sometimes we have to stand against the rules, to fight them in order to do what's right. You stood up and fought, so that earns you a pass in my book."

"Won't they just remove you and send other hunters to kill us, or return us?"

"Maybe." I say, though I know they will.

When I have allowed other creatures to stay on this planet, for the most part they went unnoticed. With the number of the Gloudians here, there's no way they'll be able to stay. Still, I need to buy some time, get my tools and weapons back before I take any sort of offensive.

"But even if you have to leave, there's still a way to save all of us from what's over there. That Porter needs to be stopped, shut down on this end so that the Hellion can't get through. But to do that, I need my bag."

"No. You need your bag so you can kill us. We're not stupid."

"There's nothing in the bag that will actually kill you. What's in there is for the lake and the portal that the Porter opened. And that's the truth."

"How can we trust you?"

He's unsure. I'm not sure I can blame him. I'm not the most honest when it comes to my job. I make promises all the time that I never plan on keeping, but this time I know what I have to do. The lake is more important than the Gloudians. They can be gathered up and killed later, but if the Hellion comes through, I'm fucked and so is the rest of the world.

"Tell me where the bag is, and then leave. I need to stop the Hellion, so while I'm dealing with the lake, you can all leave."

They seriously outnumber me, just in case they decide I'm more of a threat than they'd like. Though I think the idea of the Hellion coming through, of gathering them back up as slaves, might make help.

168

"Your bag under that thing," the Gloudian says, pointing to the overturned boat, the same one I had been hiding behind.

I can't believe it had been that close, that they hadn't taken it away from here. Probably because they had no idea what harm could come to them if they did, or because they were lazy.

"You keep your promise though and close that gate."

"I will." I say as I flip the boat over. I have never been happier to see my bag. I reach for it, but when I do, a thunderous roar explodes around me. I jump and look over to where the Gloudians are, thinking that they changed their minds or that the townspeople finally grew a set and are here to go after the strange little monsters that invaded their town.

In the end, it's neither.

It's much worse than that.

There are very few times in my life that I've been terrified. That time under the bed with the Daaf is one of them. My first date with Rouge was definitely full of fear; a different kind, but fear nonetheless. There was also a time when I was green and full of dread at what it was to be a hunter. I didn't fully understand my job when I began; I had no idea how the monsters and demons arrived, if they would be hideous or vicious.

There was no training course, no one to show me the ropes. I had to learn on the fly. Most of the creatures I came across were more sad and pathetic than dangerous. Instead of attacking, many of hid in corners and cried as I approached. With the ease of it all I started going to each job with more and more confidence. I became so sure of myself that soon I got cocky and that lead me to being sloppy. This went on for quite a while until I went in for a job at a sewage plant and was introduced to a demon called a Mauder.

I had never heard of that species before. When the man who hired me explained the problem, I went in with my gloves and a regular knife, figuring I would catch it and disable it until I found out what it really was. The man on the phone described the creature as dark and shadowy hiding near one of the holding tanks. They had called animal control first, but when it attacked a worker, they knew it was something else.

At the time, I wasn't sure what it was, and had yet to know Godfrey, so I took what I had and headed to the sewage plant. Big mistake.

A Mauder is a high level demon, a being that I should have been better equipped for and better protected against. It was like I went into shark-infested waters wearing a suit made out of chum. There were moments where I was sure I was going to die. I think I might have prayed, because I felt like I was out of options.

I was lucky and managed to get through it in one piece. I promised myself that day that I would never go into a situation unprepared and that I would never be that afraid again.

It was a promise I could never really keep.

More than half of the Gloudians are wiped out in a single motion. A huge black and green tentacle that looks almost vine-like comes out of nowhere crackling like thunder, and smashes down on the ground, crushing the small creatures. As it lifts back into the air, the survivors run, but the tentacle is too fast, and now only a handful are left alive, if that. Near two hundred Gloudians killed in seconds.

As the tentacle rises again, I'm not too surprised that it is rising out of the whirlpool and that more of the appendages are snaking out as well. It looks like the lake is giving birth to a giant octopus. I know exactly what it is.

It's the Hellion, Rector.

I turn back towards my bag and hear and feel the last of the Gloudians get crushed. They scream seconds before dying and I feel a little ashamed that I'm glad that's done, since it means I won't have to chase them down if I get done here. There is still the Porter and portal to deal with, along with the Hellion rising from it. There'll be nothing easy about what's to come.

I reach for my bag and my hand is just about to touch the strap when something wraps around my ankle. The grip is iron tight and squeezes as I'm yanked backwards towards the lake. I hit the ground hard and turn to face my fate. The lake is rapidly rising as more of the Hellion rises from the whirlpool.

He's huge. He must be as tall as a thirty-storey building. The tentacles that whip around me are connected to the demon's back. His arms, chest and head are close to humanoid, though his head is longer and there's jagged spikes along his cheeks and brow. His mouth opens and it's a huge, cavernous pit of teeth and horrible thoughts, because I'm pretty sure I'm about to go in there. Just as I'm about to hit the water, a second tentacle wraps around my chest and I'm pulled towards that waiting mouth.

This is going to hurt.

"The great monster hunter, Dillon. I was hoping to have one of them kill you before I came, but slaves aren't what they used to be," Rector growls and holds me close to his face. I'm glad he's not eating me, but to be so close to him, to smell the rot on his

171

breath and see that I might actually be shorter than one of his teeth; that's terrifying to see. "You have caused me so much grief, for someone so insignificant."

"Sorry." I sound pathetic.

"Sorry isn't a word you seem to understand, but you are going to know it well. You see, I'm going to eat you but you won't die right away. That's because when I swallow you whole, you will slowly be devoured inside of me. It could take decades. I hope it takes even longer."

"Well," I say, trying to stay cool, "I guess that's going to suck. But it won't matter. Someone else will be sent here to get you and they'll know what they're up against and how to kill you. There's no real point in staying."

"Will they send another one? Another Dillon? Oh, I doubt that very much. You are the last of your race, if I'm not mistaken. The very last Treemor. And since you are the very last of that hateful race of loathsome beasts, it doesn't really matter about any other they may send. They can send a thousand to try and kill me, but like you, they will all fail. Nothing will stop me."

I have no idea how the Hellion knows not only who I am by name, but where I originally came from. I look humanoid, as did most of my race, but I'm from a realm far from this one. A place wiped out just after I left by a war that broke out and planetary leaders that doomed my home by using every tool they could to win. I learned about its demise one hundred and ten years ago, twenty years after I arrived on earth. None of the other beings I've ever dealt with has known my past, and yet this Hellion does. And he seems to be very worried by it.

"What if there is another? Will they be able to stop you?"

"You know there are none. Your race is dead. Other than you there is no other Treemor alive. But, if one managed to stay alive and hidden, he or she can join you as you're being dissolved inside me."

The Hellion chuckles and opens his mouth, his hot breath all over me. He dangles me over rows of teeth and I struggle uselessly. He laughs. Then, in my struggles, I see a glimmer of hope.

Rouge.

She's on the beach, running towards the water with the bag in her hand. She won't know what to do with it, I didn't tell her, but I have to hope she'll figure it out. Before I get eaten would be best.

Suddenly, my weight shifts and instead of being dropped into the Hellion's mouth, I'm looking at his ugly mug again. I'm worried he saw Rouge and that he is about to squash her like he did the Gloudians. I don't know what to do. A part of me wants to yell out to open the bag and throw it in the water. If she's fast enough, maybe she can avoid getting killed. But I hesitate, because if he hasn't seen her I don't want to make to take notice. I have to hold my tongue and see what happens, keep my cool.

Damn it.

I have to keep my eyes off her.

"I'm not so sure I should eat you after all, Dillon, last of the Treemors. You have a dirty look about you and might give me problems. You've already been a pain to me here. I can only imagine what you would do in there. I've eaten little shits like you before and they give me terrible indigestion. Fifty years of that might not be such a good idea. What do you think?"

"I think that you're still afraid of me. Just like Hickner said." I try to laugh, making sure he pays attention to me and me alone.

"Afraid of you? But you're so small. Why should I be afraid of the likes of you?"

"But you are. That's why you didn't come and kill me yourself. It's why you sent the slaves to do your dirty work. You're afraid of what I can do. And you should be."

"Why? What do you know?"

There it is. He knows something about me that I don't. It could be anything. I need to figure out what it is and be fast about it.

"Are you kidding me? I'm a Treemor. You know what that means right?"

I wait, hoping I will get it out of him.

"Of course I do, but it won't matter. There's no way you'll be able to stop me."

"How can you be sure about that?" I ask as another tentacle wraps around my body, squeezing a little tighter, trapping my arms against my body.

"I have you trapped, so there's no way you can bleed on me."

My blood. How could I be so dumb and forget it?

The blood of a Treemor similar to a human's blood in many ways, but there are some properties to it that make it special in certain cases. In school, we learned that there's an enzyme in our blood, something like a protein only it's mixed with a small parasite that's harmless to my kind and almost every other race. One of my professors said that to some other creatures, particularly demons, the blood could be fatal if ingested or even touched. Our blood acts like a high-grade acid. It's been a long time since those days in school, and I had almost completely forgotten.

So Hellions are one of those species that my blood is poisonous to. But there's not much I can do about it right now. I'm all but helpless in my current state. Rector has me wrapped in his tentacles and I have no weapon to fight or even cut myself. There's not much I can do.

Unless…

A thought comes into my head, an idea so simple that it might actually work. I bite the inside of my cheek as hard as I can and the taste of copper fills my mouth. I wait a second, and then smile my biggest grin at him as I drool blood all over his ropey appendages.

At first, nothing happens. The demon's eyes move down the tentacle to where the blood lands, and then he looks back at me, almost as if he's confused that there's no pain.

Then it hits him.

Rector screams as his flesh begins to sizzle and pop. I see the blisters bubble on his flesh, until melts it away. I feel like I may get out of this alive as the vice-like grip loosens, and I fall towards the lake in what feels like slow-motion. The Hellion screams and thrashes in the water, but out of worry, I don't cry out. Instead, I call out to Rouge who is at the edge of the water.

"Throw the bag in!" I scream, but my words are like a whisper under the roar of the monster behind me.

I hit the water hard and drop right to the bottom. It's a lucky break that it's a lake with a mainly sand bottom. As I hit, I avoid most of the rocks scattered there and the softness allows me to recover fast. I go to push up, to drive myself back to the surface, but grab a rock first because I have an idea. Once I have one in hand, I rush back to the surface. It's getting hard to breathe and I break through as my lungs burn mercilessly.

At first I'm disoriented. The day is losing light and I try to figure which way to go; towards shore, or towards the Hellion. My decision is made easy when I see the giant monster striding towards me. Guess I'm dealing with him first.

"I'll tear you to shreds!" Rector screams, his body is cutting easily through the water. His remaining tentacles swirl over his head and I'm sure he's going to try and squash me like he did the Gloudians. But if does, no doubt that he will get more of my blood on him, which I doubt he wants. Yet that's not stopping him from coming at me, which is fine by me because I know what I want to do.

I do my best to tread water and then use one hand to hit myself in the head with the rock; hard.

Once.

Twice.

It takes a third and then a fourth strike before I feel blood running down my face. I give the wound two more shots, wanting to make sure the blood is really flowing and as I do, I see the Hellion slow, as though it can tell what I'm doing. I look down at the water and see it darkening. It's working. I drop the rock and start to swim towards him, ready to let the red touch his skin. I want to burn a hole right through the bastard.

I think Rector gets what I am going to do because he stops quickly and then turns back towards the whirlpool, moving away faster than he had been charging at me. I should have waited to open myself up. I should have let him get closer before doing it.

176

He's way too big for me to catch up to him, but I have to try. I push my body as hard as I can, swimming as fast as possible, but he's already close to the whirlpool. He's going to get away. He's going to go through the portal and that will be that. I'm about to lose my chance to kill him and avoid him opening another portal.

Damn it.

I'm already too late.

The Hellion is at the whirlpool already and is starting to submerge. In seconds he will be gone, back to where he came from and all hope of killing him will be lost. I stop and want to scream, but what's the point? I see his head sinking back down, almost completely out of sight. He's going to be gone in moments. I wait and watch for it to happen, cursing myself for acting too quickly.

But he doesn't go under all the way. He's stopped moving.

Cautiously I begin to swim towards him again. I wipe blood away from my eyes and then he comes flying back up out of the water and I think I've been had. He was luring me to him, and now he's going to attack. His plan was to get me close to the portal so he could throw me through, not kill me here at all. I have no idea where he's from, but if that's his plan, I'm sure there will be other creatures and more Gloudians there waiting for my arrival.

I get ready for him to come at me, to grab or attack.

Only he doesn't do anything at all. That might be because only half his body floats on the surface. The rest of him, chest down, is missing. Then, a second body, small and human looking, rises out of the water. Even from this distance I'm able to see the swirls on his chest, deep cuts that belong to a Porter; the key to opening a portal.

I'm confused.

"Dillon!"

I turn back to the shore and see Rouge in the water. She's coming for me. I look back at the bodies, wanting to be reassured that the Hellion is dead, and then swim to her.

"Are you okay?" she asks, no doubt seeing all the blood.

"Yeah. I think so. You?"

"I'm fine. But what the fuck just happened?"

I'm about to tell her I have no idea until the moment I see she's in the water with the bag. She had no idea what to do with the items, but she did it anyway. The bag has the tools to close the portal, so when she entered the water, they worked right away and must have killed the Porter. And since Rector was in the midst of going through the portal, he was cut in two when it closed.

I laugh as I get to her and kiss her. "Looks like you saved my ass again."

"Really?"

"I'll explain when we get back to shore."

We swim back, slowly, as I'm bone tired and sore. We get back and I tell her how she saved me without even knowing it.

"That's just how good I am." She chuckles and we lay on the sand for a moment.

It's a good moment. The sun is almost gone and the first stars are just starting to glimmer. If I wasn't bleeding and surrounded by a bunch of dead monsters and infected townspeople, this might actually be romantic. In a way, I guess it still is, especially with Rouge around.

"Is your job always this exciting?" she asks.

"I try not to let things get this out of hand. I hope this is a one-off really, but you never know."

"I think next time I'll be a little more patient and just wait for you to get back to the city. I think my days of monster hunting are over."

"Can't blame you there." I laugh and am happy to hear her referring to a next time. Part of me worried that when we got out of this in one piece that it would be it for us. I'm luckier today than I have ever been in my life.

We lay there quietly for a while. She takes my hand, giving it a squeeze now and then. I would love to close my eyes and have a nap, but I can't. There may still be Gloudians in town, not to mention infected. I wish I could say it's all over, but I know it's not. Not quite yet.

"Can I ask you something, Dillon?"

"Sure."

"What's a Treemor?"

Shit. "You heard that, did you?"

"I heard a lot, really. After you were taken from city hall and pulled down the street, I couldn't just sit and watch. I had to find you and do what I could. I think I was pretty stealthy too. I didn't get noticed at all. I got here just as you were telling the little blue and yellow things to fight back and saw the whole attack from that giant green thing. Then I heard him call you a Treemor. Does that mean you're not really human?"

This sucks. Never thought I would like a human girl, let alone have strong feelings for one. I had no intention of telling her that I was a monster myself, but she heard and there's no point in lying, is there?

"Well, no. I'm not human. Sorry."

She turns her head to look at me and I do the same. She smiles as she squeezes my hand.

"I'm not surprised you're not human. You're way too cool for that."

I laugh and she gives me a punch on the arm.

"Ow. What's that for?"

"You just laughed at me."

"I'm not laughing at you. I'm laughing because I thought you were going to say something like, 'I'm not surprised you're not human because sex with you was out of this world'."

"Really? You thought I would say that?" She mocks offense. "Listen, Dillon, if you ever want to get into my panties again, you better get to know me a little better than that. Dad jokes and lame ass one liners are my thing. Not that cheese."

"I'll try to remember that."

Rouge moves closer and rests her head on my chest. I relax a little for the first time since our first night here. She whispers to me as we lie there—things I will keep private for now—but they were enough to put a smile on my face.

It's going to be nice to get home, and I hope I'll never have to see this town again for as long as I live.

FRIDAY

It's well after midnight now and it's high time the two of us get moving. At some point I must have passed out. I know that seems like a bad idea, but since nothing came after us while we lay there, I assume that there's nothing to worry about. If any Gloudians or infected townspeople are left, they probably want to stay far away from me at this point.

After we wipe the sand from us, Rouge checks my head and winces. "How the hell did you do that to yourself?"

"I'm tenacious," I chuckle and heft the bag off the ground.

I open the bag and look inside. What's in there is good for closing a portal, but there's no weapons, so I close it again. When I get back to the city I'll return it to Godfrey and thank him for saving my ass.

"So now what? Should we get to the hotel, grab our stuff and get the hell out of dodge?"

"Not yet. It's not over."

"You're kidding, right?"

"No. But this shouldn't be nearly as crazy or dangerous as the Hellion you killed, so it's a walk in the park."

"Yeah, a walk in a park that's full of psycho killers."

"How about I drop you at the motel, and you can wait until I get done. No need for you to do any more than you have."

"And what if I need to save your ass again, Dillon? No, I think it'd be better if I stayed with you."

I nod and we walk away from the lake. We have to be careful

not to slip in the mess of the dead that covers the parking lot. Severed body parts, mashed Gloudians and the eviscerated infected are scattered everywhere. I see Rouge wince as she steps over the head of a woman whose eyes stare blankly at the night sky, and accidentally crunches the fingers of a Gloudian instead. I laugh because I can't help it.

If you had told me a week ago that I would be walking through a battlefield in a small town with a woman I loved, I would have told you to check into a psych ward. It seems impossible, but as she reaches to take my hand, she reminds me of how real it all is.

"Now that's a lucky break," I say, reaching down to the body of an infected.

He's cut in two, but that doesn't bother me as I pull my knives from his belt and my gloves from his pocket. "These will help."

"I'll take your word for it."

I think about how long the walk to city hall will be until my eyes fall on my car, unharmed aside from some blood spatter. What a break.

The streets are dark and very quiet. In the woods I hear animals moving, but that's about it. We drive slowly, ready for anything, but even when we get back to Main Street, there's not a soul. Not a Gloudian, not one infected; nothing. Not even a regular townie. I'm not sure if it's a good or bad thing.

"Where are we going?" Rouge asks as we pass a dried pool of blood where Preston was killed.

"City Hall," I say as I drive towards it.

Ever since I woke up on the beach, my mind has been focused on the mayor of this city. The bastard that offered me up to the Hellion. There's nothing I need more than to find him, and then gut him like the pig he is.

I don't tell Rouge this, and I'm sure as hell not going to let her sit in the room while I do it. Sometimes my line of work gets pretty messy and can be pretty damn disturbing. But I know it needs to be done, if only for shits and giggles.

He murdered Hank Gibson. The image of Hank being decapitated has been in my head ever since we left the beach. I would like to return the favour to Mayor Fent.

I park the car and hand Rouge the keys.

"Why are you giving them to me?" She holds them out as if she doesn't want them.

"If you need to get out of here in a hurry, I want you to get out. I'd feel better if you have them."

"I thought you said this was going to be no big deal?"

"After what this town has thrown at me, I'd rather play it safe."

She pockets the keys. We find the doors of city hall unlocked. Good. I remember that Gibson said the mayor sometimes sleeps here. Inside the building all the lights are out. It's not so unusual, but the hairs on the back of my neck stand up. Something is wrong, like a bad smell, or a strange chill in the air, but I can't pick what it is.

"Nobody's here, Dillon."

"Doesn't seem like it."

I'm not so sure she's right. I don't see anyone, but I feel that there is someone here; close. It's like there are eyes on me right now.

"Should we just go then?"

"No. We'll wait here until the morning."

I don't think we'll need to wait until morning to find out what's here.

"What are you planning on doing to him when you find him?"

"I'm…" I stop. There's a noise up ahead and then I see it; a light under the mayor's office door. Bingo!

"What?" she asks, not seeing what I do.

"Right there." I point at the door. "That's probably him, no doubt waiting for the Hellion to come to him. I doubt he has any idea what's happened. Now I need you to do me a favour."

"Let me guess, you want the helpless girl to run and hide in the washroom again? Or should I go to the car?" she asks.

I can tell by the tone of her voice that she doesn't want to leave me. I don't want her to leave me either, but I can't let her see me with Fent.

"I don't think you're helpless. But there are things I need to do that I'd rather you not see. "

"Please don't get hurt." I hear the hesitation in her voice.

"I'll do my best. Where will you go?"

"I'll hide in the bathroom again. If I hear any sort of trouble I'm out of here. But don't get hurt, and please hurry. I want to get the hell out of this place."

"Fast as I can." I say and kiss her.

I'm lying. After all that Fent has done—getting me here, setting me up to die, endangering Rouge and murdering

Gibson—I'm going to make the bastard suffer. But I don't say that to her, so I lie and seal it with a kiss that I hope makes it all right. As I pull away, she hugs me. For a second I don't think she's going to let go, but then her grip loosens.

"Stay safe, lover."

"I'll do my best."

I watch her walk away. Once she starts to walk down the stairs, I turn back towards the door and pull out my knives.

Time to go to work.

I open the door fast and see I was wrong. Fent is there with Gibson's body, but nothing is right with the place. Fent looks off behind his desk. He's not as fat as I remember, nor as solid for that matter. I don't even need to touch him to see what the problem is.

He's empty.

What's sitting behind the desk is a husk, a skin suit of the man I had met the other day. When I touch his flesh, it falls forward and a milky blood oozes out of his empty mouth and eyes. The husk that is still warm, so whatever happened to him, happened recently.

I pull the empty mayor back up and look at him, trying to figure out what happened to him. It's as though some creature has sucked the bone, blood and muscle from him. But what would have done it, and why? I can't think of a single creature who has handiwork like this.

There's nothing else in the room with me, no monster or demon scent. Everything seems normal, aside from the man suit. I say it seems normal, but there has been little in the way of normal since I arrived. Even the nutjob Preston said that something seemed off. Preston had mentioned strange, dark and out of place. Some human looking being that might have…

Oh shit!

What I'm thinking now is almost ridiculous, but that would sum up this whole job. There have been rumours and whispers as far back as I can remember, almost myth and legend, about a species simply known as the Shadow People. As the tales go, they are a dark sort, as though made up of gaps the light doesn't hit. When they want, they enter another being and take over the body, feeding slowly on the muscle, blood and bone. I had always thought it a story people go on about like Bigfoot or vampires. Thinking they could be real was a little like trying to believe in Santa Claus. But when I look back at the shell that was Fent, it is the only thing that makes sense.

The question is how long was one inside him? Did Fent bringing me here, and work with the Hellion? Was the mayor I met ever really the mayor?

And if there was a shadow inside Fent, where is it now?

If the rumours about the Shadow People are true, they never go anywhere alone. And right now, a group of Shadow People are not something I want to deal with. The idea was to kill Fent and get the hell out of this town. With Fent dead, there's only splitting left.

I need to get Rouge and get the hell out of here.

As if on cue, a scream echoes through the hallways and my blood runs cold.

"DILLON!"

It's Rouge. I run out of the office and pray I can get to her while she is still herself.

"DILLON, HELP ME!"

In seconds I'm down the stairs and in the dark hallway. It's hard to see, but there's Rouge with darkness spread over her arms and throat.

"Dillon the Monster Dick. The pleasure is ours," I hear coming from her direction, a faint voice that slithers.

"Let her go," I tell the thing that I can barely see.

"Why should we? Such a lovely body, such warm insides. She would fit any one of us so nicely. A body that would be as delicious from the inside as it looks on the outside."

My eyes are adjusting and I can see them a little better. Almost human-like shapes, one behind her, holding her, and others on either side.

"Don't hurt her, please," I beg.

With myths and legends, you hear a lot of stories about how to kill them, but who knows if any of them are true. If you were to run into an actual vampire, would a stake kill them, or the sun, some silver? Or are they all stories?

I have heard that the sun will kill a Shadow Person; also that iron will, some curses, a Reath from Torror; but I have none of those items on me anyway. All I have is my willingness to do whatever it takes to protect Rouge.

"It will only hurt for a moment. There is a bit of cold, then a little pain and then only oblivion. She'll be long dead before she is eaten from the inside out."

"Jesus Christ, Dillon. Get me the fuck out of here," Rouge screams, looking as scared as I feel.

"What do you want? What can I give you so that you'll let her go?"

"Ah, a bargain. I do so love a good bargain. Well, what would I like? How about the body of the very last Treemor alive? Your kind was always strong and filling, not like these humans really. They lack the long lasting tastes that your kind always provided."

"Is that what this is all about? Why I was brought to town? So you could take my body?"

"Oh no. We had nothing to do with this. We were in the bodies of three Gloudians when we found out about the Hellion. When we realized he was after you, a Treemor, well, we just couldn't resist. So we came here and have let things play out."

"What if I had been killed by the Hellion, or the Gloudians, or even the hybrids?"

"It would have been regretful, but we never had a doubt that you would come out on top. We know your reputation. Of course, there are always things that have to be left to chance. And if you died, we were more than ready to take the Hellion. He would have been an equally satisfying treat. But here we are and you're still alive, which suits us just fine."

I'm speechless. I don't know what I can do, but I have to protect Rouge. Since I came to Earth, I have never had someone I cared about in my life. I look at her face and can see how scared she is and that tears at me.

A week ago, I was just Dillon. A loner and a hunter; nothing more. The only thing that mattered was my job and watching HBO on Sundays. Now I have her, someone I will die for if that's what it takes.

"Let her go then, and you can have me," I say.

"No, Dillon!" Rogue cries out, but she won't change my mind.

"Why should we let her go? We can just as easily have her and then take you. There's nothing stopping us from having it all."

"There is."

I pull my knife out and press the blade hard against my throat, feeling it cut into me. Warm blood runs down my neck. I think I have their attention.

Or at least I hope it has.

"Well, this is interesting."

"Let her go, or I kill myself. You may get her, but your chances of having me, the last Treemor will be gone."

"We can't allow that, brother," one says to the others.

"No, we can't," another speaks up.

"Since none of us have personally had the pleasure of tasting a Treemor before, and you are the last, we'd rather not waste such a fine opportunity," The first agrees and turns back to me. "What do you suggest?"

"Let her go. When she's out of the building, I'll drop the knife and you will be able to do whatever it is you want."

The three of them whisper to one another. I catch parts, enough for me to know that they're going for it. They have to. For them, it's a once in a lifetime chance.

The two holding Rouge let her go and she runs right to me. Her body slams into me so hard I end up cutting my neck more deeply, but it's nice to feel her against me and as she kisses my lips, the sting of the blade fades.

"You don't have to do this, Dillon. You have to be able to fight them," she whispers in my ear.

"Not this time. There's no other way."

"They'll kill you."

"Better they have me than they take you. I couldn't let that happen. Here," I say and kiss her again, "when you get back to the city, take the bag in the car back to Godfrey and let him know what happened. Let him know that these things are here and not to trust me if he should see me again."

"Please, Dillon. There has to be a way out of this."

"Not that I can think of. Now go. Before they change their minds."

"I can't!"

"You have to. Do it for me. I love you," I say and before she can say anything, I kiss her on the lips for what might be the last time. When I pull away, I see she's crying.

"You're a real jerk, Dillon, you know that? First cool guy I ever meet and fall for, and you go and get yourself killed."

"Sorry."

"Yeah. Me too."

She kisses me hard again and whispers in my ear that she loves me too. My knees feel a bit weak, but when she pulls away I stay strong and smile at her, hoping I don't give away how close to crying I am.

"Now, go." I tell her.

She heads towards the main doors and before she disappears, she gives me one last look.

Then, she's gone and safe.

Now it's time to fulfill my end of the bargain.

The Shadow People are inching towards me, despite the fact that I still have the knife to my throat. They move like ghosts, dark shapes that glide along the ground. As they get closer, I can see their lack of detail; they look like a two-dimensional shadow rather than anything real, though their eyes blink and their mouth opens and shuts.

"Now, Dillon," one of them says as they creep towards me, "I think it's time you put the knife down, don't you? She's safe. We kept up our end of the bargain."

He's right. I lower the knife slowly and wait for what comes next, but my mind is still trying to find a way out of this, and I have an idea. Not a great one, but it worked with the Gloudians, maybe it will work here too. If I can work them off against each other, I'm free.

"So are you three going to fight over me? Since there's only one of me and three of you, how are you going to decide who gets me?"

"That's easy, Dillon. None of us needs to fight to have you. We all will."

"Maybe your life on Earth has taken away your ability to see things differently. We are not individuals here; we are all part of a bigger, greater life. We will join and become one to feast on you."

Shit. That didn't work.

I try and figure out some other way to get out of it, but the three shadows merge in a split second and before I can move, run, they're in me.

I guess this is the end of Dillon the Monster Dick.

The cold is like being naked in a frozen lake, but somehow worse. I feel my skin tighten all over and want to scream as every nerve ending in my body explodes in white-hot frozen fire. My fists clench and I feel as though my body is going into a seizure.

Then, the room begins to dim and the pain starts to drain

away as suddenly as it started. This is must be what death feels like. I've dished it out before, I guess it was only a matter of time before it was served back to me.

Meh, I've felt worse.

Death isn't so bad. It's quiet, and dark, and there is a sense of peace that I've never really known. It's better than sleep; almost totally relaxing. I feel as though I am nothing more than air floating free. I can sense things around me, like I am surrounded by others I once knew. I can't see them, but I know they're there in the darkness.

I even sense Rouge.

All those fears of death now seem trite. It's like as soon as the darkness overcame me, I understood it all. Life, death and all the junk in-between. Beliefs I once had are shattered. What I could never grasp become crystal clear. And it's then that I see that my death will be short lived. There is something about me that is about to kill the Shadow People that are trying to kill me. I guess I'm not totally dead after all.

I'm on my knees vomiting when the darkness bleeds away. The hall is still black, but not the same density as it was. Another wave of nausea washes over me and I open my mouth to puke. What comes out isn't partially digested food or bile; it's an inky slime. All that's left of my body's invaders, at a guess. The

192

Shadow People puked out like a bad burrito. They taste horrible as they bubble out my nose and pool under me.

As I heave again, I try not to laugh as my eye catches sight of my exposed wrist and know what it was that saved me. For the second time in as many days, my tattoos and brandings have come in handy—the one closest to my right thumb is glowing a strange amber.

I should count myself lucky that they hadn't noticed my tattoos and scarification. They protect me against common spirits and demons, but I never thought of the Shadow People as either of those. They were more myth. And since the tales only talk about relics and physical things destroying them, I'd never considered that what would work on others would work on them.

Allowing them to take me to protect Rouge in the end was the best thing I could have done.

The last of the black stuff seems to be out. I stand up, and my body is arthritically sore. With a groan and stretch, I grab my knives and get out of there. My mouth tastes like burnt hair, and I keep spitting, hoping to get the taste of the dirty bastards out of my mouth. I wish I had gum on me.

I have no idea how much time has passed, but I hope to hell Rouge hasn't left the motel. I run as fast as I can through quiet streets. I don't bother to see if anyone is peeking out from their windows or if the infected are shuffling about. All I want to do is get to her.

I'm less than half a mile from the motel when I see headlights approaching. I think it's my car, but I can't be certain. The car is not steady, the lights move back and forth across the horizon. Rouge has told me she doesn't drive so I pray that it's her and get off the road. When the car gets closer, I wave my arms wildly and the tires screech across the asphalt as my car as it skids sideways, looking as though it's coming right at me. That would be just my luck today. With everything else that I've fought through and survived, I would die by getting hit by my own car. Driven by a woman I love. That would be the icing on the cake.

Luckily the car stops before it hits me and Rouge is behind the wheel, eyes wide and staring. I wave and she fumbles with something in the passenger's seat before she finally gets out of the car. I'm expecting a hug and kiss, but instead she comes charging at me with Godfrey's baseball bat, which is not really a bat at all. I stumble backwards and raise my hands.

"Whoa!" I cry as she swings the bat wildly. "Rouge, what the hell are you doing? It's me."

"Sure it is. You're in there, you bastards. You stole him from me and now you're coming to get me. I swear to God if you come near me I will brain you."

"Rouge. It's just me. I promise."

"Bullshit."

"Do you remember what I whispered to you before you left?"

"You said a lot of things."

"But only one that really mattered. And, it's true. I do. Not just because I nearly got you killed or because you saved my ass. Every message you sent me, every time you hugged me or even touched my hand I felt something I've never felt before. And that's saying a lot."

"How do I know it's really you? How do I know one of them isn't in you and just feeding off your thoughts?"

"You don't, I guess. But look at me and maybe you'll see that it's really me."

194

I can't blame her for being cautious; I would be too. But I have to prove to her that it's me. If not, she's either going to smash my head in with that bat, or she'll never see me again. I don't like either of those options. "I have no real way to make you believe it is me, but I'll try anything. If I have to, I'll prove it in bed. Show you that I'm so good in bed, I'm out of this world."

Rouge groans and I laugh.

"I should beat your skull in just for saying that again," she says, but drops the bat instead and runs to me. I hold her tight and feel her melt into me. "Can we please leave this fucking town now?"

"We have just one more thing to do."

"What?"

"I'm kidding. Let's hit the road."

I've never been so happy to end a job.

Only, who's going to pay me for this?

AUTHOR'S NOTE

This is the first book in the Dillon the Monster Dick series. I have already written a few short stories, and there are keys to this story in all of them. You don't have to read them to understand *The Gate At Lake Drive*, but if you do, I think there is a clearer road to what is going on. Again, you don't have to read them, but if you were to, start with *The Undergarment Eater,* which you'll find in *Dark Eclipse,* Issue 29 and *Dark Reaches*, and which has been reproduced immediately after this note in this book.

As for the story itself, I want to start off apologizing to the people of the real town of Innisfil. What appears in this book is no way a representation of that town or the people that live there. This is pure fiction and I only used the name as a backdrop, not as source material.

I've been to Innisfil many times, as my aunt used to live there too and if you visit, you will see that nothing in the book appears in the town, other than Lake Simcoe. So some people might ask why I used the name of a real town when I could have made up a town that shared the same shoreline. Personally, I love to read a book that uses a backdrop of a city or better yet, a town I know, even if it isn't accurate. It's just cool to read one that mentions a place I know or visit, often that most people might not know about. I'm not trying to bad mouth the town or give it a bad name. This is fiction. I remade the world so that it suited my story better. Anyone who has read my short, *Shutdown,* will know that I did the same thing for Toronto. The story is the only thing that can dictate where a building will or won't stand, which direction a road will go and sometimes the stores and landmarks that may or may not exist there.

Being a writer can be fun that way.

I hope that if you read this book, and the short stories, you like Dillon as a character. I have plans for at least six more books with him, maybe more, as well as collecting all the short stories I plan to write in one edition that will be on chronological order of events. The next book to follow will be *Earthbound and Down*, which is already in the works.

Let's see where this goes.

Shaun Meeks

Toronto, Ontario April 2014

Bonus Short Story: The Undergarment Eater

The blood that ran into my eyes from the superficial head wound made it hard to see, but I had to concentrate, needed to stay focused. The little bastard that had thrown part of the bleachers at me and caused this wound was still somewhere in the gymnasium. I could hear the subtle sounds of its movements in the darkness, so I knew I wasn't out of danger just yet. I softened my breath, struggled to make it as quiet as possible to keep my position a secret for as long as I could, hoping it would be enough. Through the dark, from my vantage point, I tried to see some sign of where the blasted thing had gone. I wiped away some of the blood, thought how stupid it was that a cut that was little more than a scratch could bleed so damn much. Where did you go you, you little bastard?

Fear should have made my heart beat so rapidly that it threatened to blow, but monsters stalking me in the dark was nothing new to me. In fact, I made it my goal to find myself in strange and terrifying places, looking for and confronting the things that people only think of as nightmare. I had once found a serpent, not your average snake, but a two thousand year old being that had chosen to live in a serpentine body and fed on babies that slept in cribs. It may have gone on living another two thousand years or more if it hadn't started eating kids. If it had just stayed out of sight and kept a low profile, nobody would have been any the wiser, but these creatures had a way of losing control after a while.

The week before the gym, I had been in the basement of a church where in the wine cellar I had come face to face with a monster made of dirt and refuse. The creature had tunneled its way up into one of the confessionals where it fed on the dispelled sins of the parishioners. For that one, the church had been reluctant to allow me in to investigate, not one to believe in the supernatural despite their tales of zombies and men that have super human strength due to their long hair.

It wasn't the first time I have been called into a church. For some reasons many of the demons and monsters I deal with have an affinity for them. Like humans, these beings hold on to old ways and nostalgia, and flock to places they heard talk about on their origin world.

Eventually, the church had let me in, after escalating numbers of tales from their flock, and what I found was a pathetic little creature who was over six thousand years old and named was Gus. Old Gus didn't put up much of a fight, and in the end said quite solemnly, "I wouldn't mind seeing what comes next anyway. I wonder if I will return home or end up somewhere else." I gave him his wish and relieved him of whatever life the little dirt monster had on Earth.

This one in the gym, the one hidden in the shadows that had already cut me and stalked me, didn't want to go away as easily. When I finally cornered it in the gymnasium of the local high school an hour or so ago, by locking all doors and windows, sealing them with spells that would keep them that way until I removed them, that was when the creature lashed out and attacked.

I had been contacted by the school principal through my website; the man looked a little like a shaved bear with his full face, ample belly and thick, paw like hands. The principal was not sure what to do about the strange rumours and incidents in the halls of the school. Students and teachers had told tales of a creature in the bathrooms and change rooms; a dark, almost human shaped thing that came up through the toilets, usually content with stealing socks and underwear, that had recently begun attacked students and maintenance workers. There were pictures showing where the thing's clawed hand had torn through a shirt, two pairs of pants and the flesh of a janitor's arm. I studied the pictures, seeing if I could decipher from the wounds what it was, but nothing I had ever seen or read about seemed to fit. I told the principal that I would take the job, and asked that all students and staff be kept out of the building until I was done.

Hiding behind some of the wreckage in the huge gym, I wondered if by done, I had meant my own death. At the time I hadn't, but things were not going as smoothly as I would have liked. When I had first found it in the boys change room, it was greedily sucking and chewing on a handful of old underwear. I surprised it, and then chased it into the gym, having already set the room up with spells to trap it, sure that the encounter would end quickly. But this creature had other things in mind.

As I approached, watching the unknown monster with vibrant blue and yellow skin that shifted its markings with each step, I wondered what I would use to kill it. A spell? One of my powers? Or maybe just brute force? I had thought of just grabbing hold of it and wringing the little weasel's neck, as I had done to others from time to time.

The thing sat huddled on the bleachers, hissing at my approach like it was a cat, huge black eyes staring at me with fear and anger. I mentally searched through my experiences to figure out what was before me, but I didn't know. With these situations, you had to use the right tool to extinguish the creature or it could get, well, messy.

I cautiously approached the crouching creature, studying it as I went, in hopes of figuring out what it was and where it was from. As I did, something began to happen to it.

The bright vibrant colours of its skin began to fluctuate, appearing as though they were evaporating upwards until they were completely gone and the being before me turned to a dark charcoal.

Well, I've never seen that before.

The now slick, black creature continued to hiss at me as I walked across the shiny wood floor. More than likely it had known that it was cornered and about to be expelled from Earth, back to whatever realm it had come from.

"So, you want to tell me who you are? Where you come from? Give me a little hint before you go? Before you die."

At the words die, the creature reacted.

Its mouth opened wide and it let out a shriek that threatened to pop my eardrums. I covered my ears as it howled, and began to thrash against the wooden bleachers. I began backing away as I saw wood splinter and lucky that I did, as the creature began to tear up huge chunks of it and throwing them. The creature threw huge pieces of the destroyed bleachers at me and up at the lights, smashing them all so that the gym was left in darkness. Some of the pieces that crashed around me were ten times bigger than the thing that had thrown them, letting me know that whatever the creature was, it was a strong one. Stronger than most I had faced.

Why couldn't you be more like the Tissue Man?

The Tissue Man was a demon—well, more of a demon's underling that had escaped its realm and decided to hide in the suburbs of Markham, just outside of Toronto. This demon had believed in Catholic dogma, truly thought that it was a servant of Satan and when it formed its physical body in our plane, it had for some unknown reason called forth the sins of young boys on one particular street. From the bedrooms of these teenagers, happy tissues full of wasted nights in front of a computer screen or dreams of that girl that had ignored them, found their way to the hiding demon, and made up his physical form. It would have been content to hide in the dark, live in the shadows and just watch human life as some are apt to do, but when the demon had called forth the crumpled tissues, when it had whispered the incantation from the safety of its new home, it had no idea how sexually verbose the young males on that street were.

Tissue after tissue found the demon, making him grow larger and larger so that he was unable to stay hidden from people. I had been called by a one of the fathers on the street, having heard of my services on the internet, after the man had been walking his dog late one night and saw the Tissue Man hiding between two houses.

"I smelled something weird, something I recognize, but I couldn't place. My dog started barking and that's when I saw it. I think it may be the ghost of a giant."

As it turned out it wasn't, though I joked later that it could be considered a ghost; one made up of all the fallen soldiers the teenagers had deposited into the tissues, and then tossed in the waste basket.

I had shown up two days after speaking to the father and found the demon's hiding place. It was an unused septic tank in the backyard of a foreclosed house at the end of the street. I had seen the demon going in and out, following its scent to track it. Once it had left the tank, I set up a trap, and waited. I hid in bushes for over an hour until the crumpled, white tissue demon returned. When it entered the lair, the one I had already doused in gasoline, it didn't stand a chance. I ran over, tossed my Zippo in and flames exploded upwards. The best way to despatch a demon, especially one that holds onto the traps of what people think of as Hell, is with fire.

From inside the tank, the demon wailed. I looked down for a second, catching a glimpse of it thrashing and a quick whiff of burning tissues, jizz and shit before I slammed the lid of the tank closed, sealed it with a spell and left the demon to die.

It had been an easy job, unlike the thing from the gym.

I wiped more blood from my forehead, trying to keep it out of my eyes as I hid behind a large section of the bleachers off to one side of the gym. I peered around the corner, tried to see if the creature loomed close by, but when I looked, there was only darkness and the shadows of destruction. I clenched my fists and felt rage build up inside me. I hated that I had allowed the thing to get the upper hand on me, feeling as though the little creature, the panty eater, had been no real threat to me. When I had heard the stories, seen the photos and then actually seen the creature that I could not identify at all, it should have been enough to encourage me to act with caution, to fall back a little and assess the situation. I had allowed my cockiness, my history of having an easy time with monsters, demons and otherworldly creatures, to cloud my judgement. I had not considered how bad things could go. I should have thought on past situations that had gone bad, instead of relying on my recent luck. I shouldn't have looked at its small size as a sign of weakness.

I pondered briefly, as I hid behind the wreckage and listened for any sounds from the creature, just how long I had been in the business for. It seemed like many lifetimes ago that I had decided to take on the task of hunting down beings that had no right to exist in the current reality I was in.

Despite my appearance, I was an old and experienced man in the game, so I should have known better than to walk in without a solid game plan. I suppose I had a game plan, but it turns out that it wasn't all that good. Corner it and kill it. That was as far as I had gotten.

When the principal had reached out to me through my website, it had seemed like a simple job. It had sounded like one where I'd be in and out, get my pay and return home in a few hours. When I had shown up at the school, I had met the principal in the parking lot, with the school already clear of students and staff.

"Thank you for coming, Mister…"

"Just Dillon. No mister with me."

"What is your title with the church then?"

Always with that. People tended to think that I had some affiliation with the church, some church, any church, but that was not so. They all thought they were dealing with monsters and demons from Hell, but Hell in the sense that they knew it didn't exist. I wondered what they would say and think if I told them the truth, told them who I really was, or where those things really came from. I doubted that any sane person would remain that way if they knew the truth, so I only said what they wanted to hear.

Ignorance is bliss.

"The church doesn't really have a title for me. It's why I have the website. They would rather keep this all off the record; nobody wants this kind of thing to go public. The church has enough problems. I'm sort of like the CIA of the church; I don't exist."

The principle laughed nervously and went on to explain where the creature was last seen. I thanked him and told him I would call the cell number given when the creature was dead and the school was safe. Without saying goodbye, I went into the school after it. I pulled out a piece of gum and chewed as I walked through the door, expecting a cake walk, but that was before I had been hit in the head with a piece of shredded bleacher and found myself squatting in the darkness.

There was movement to my right. My head shot in that direction and I thought I saw a shadow dart just out of my sight line. I moved slowly in that direction, careful not to shift anything or breathe too heavily. Before I had crawled more than three feet, though, something pounced on my back.

And hissed.

I grunted and felt burning across my back as the thing dug claws into my flesh, gripping on before doing anything else. I cursed at it, stood up quickly and tried to reach back and pull the damned thing free. The claws dug deeper into me, warm blood trickling down my back and I did the only thing I could think to do.

I quickly spun around so that my back was facing the wall, and then ran backwards at full speed, crashing into the painted cinderblock. I heard the creature on me scream out like an animal as it was crushed between the wall and two hundred pounds of meat and bone. The claws immediately disengaged from my back and I moved quickly, turning as the creature crashed to the floor. I pressed my booted foot against the thing's throat and took out my gloves from the pocket of my coat. The leather gloves woven with silver, gold and platinum were important when dealing with these things. Spellbound with every charm known, they made even the greatest foe unable to fight back.

Once they were on, I reached down and grabbed the creature that was pinned to the floor, lifting it off the ground. For something so little, no more than three feet tall, it weighed quite a bit. But I needed to find out what this being was, where it was from and I needed light to do so.

The creature still tried to fight, giving a quick, violent thrash here and there as I took it to the change room, and that surprised me. Normally, when the gloves touched some demon that thought it was a total bad ass, or moved to the center of a spectre where the solid essence of it hid, they lost all will to fight or even move. Somehow, this little creature had enough spunk in it to withstand them. They were new gloves though; my older pair sat at home partially damaged and Godfrey had sworn the replacements would be just as good.

I wonder if Godfrey ripped me off with these ones. Maybe left out a spell or two.

That wouldn't surprise me in the least. In all the years I had been dealing with Godfrey, buying his special wares and goods, there was always something a bit shady about him. There was always a smile playing on his lips as though he knew some great secret that he would never share with anyone else, that brought him some sort of joy. Either that or he knew that what he was selling were half assed artifacts that might or might not be fully functional when the time came to using them and Godfrey found it funny. I would need to stop by and speak to him when I was wrapped up with this little bastard.

I pushed my way into the boy's change room, and once in the light, I looked down at the creature in my hands. The thing was staring up at me, baring yellowish, daggered teeth and hissing repeatedly like a cat. It was ugly, somewhat like a fish that had eyes too big for its head. The skin was still the dark charcoal colour, though flecks of the yellow and blue rippled across the creatures flesh now and again. I had never seen anything like it before.

Normally the demons and monsters I dealt with were made up of items from this world. Since these beings were not part of this world, they need to borrow things to walk around in it, to make them whole and visible. They left their bodies behind when they crossed over, entering our world in a strange, floating globe form. Even the spectres pulled gases like car exhaust and chemical fumes to form their mist-like bodies. Yet this thing looked the way they would look in their own world, something I had never seen before.

I took it over to the bathroom area and slammed it down hard on the sink.

"Now, this can go one of two ways, hard or really hard. How would you like it?"

The thing only hissed again, specks of spittle flying from its mouth and hitting my gloves.

"Are you saying you don't understand me? That you can't speak? If that's the case, I guess I'll just have to do this for fun." I reached over and turned on the tap while keeping the thing pinned down with the other other hand, and then pulled my weapon from my jacket. At first glance, it looked like a knife, made of brass or something close to it, but as the creature looked at it, saw the carvings on it and engraved spells, it knew that what I was holding was a Tincher; a torture tool used to flay creatures well protected against mortal blades.

"Wait. Don't! I do understand. What do you want to know?"

I smiled, knowing that the threat of pain and torture always made tight lips loosen. I placed the blade under the water, letting the spells absorb what was needed to work, and then held it close to the creature.

"Let's start with who and what you are?"

"My name is Hickner, and I'm a Gloudian."

"What the fuck is a Gloudian?"

"I thought you were a hunter, shouldn't you know? I thought your race was trained to know everything." The creature smirked, but it was short lived as I touched his flesh with the tip of the blade, making a small cut. Hickner howled in pain and I was sure I had gotten the point.

No pun intended.

"Let's not mess around here, Hickner. I want some answers, not fucking games. I've never heard of that race before, because it doesn't exist. Tell me what the hell you are or this is going to go very badly for you. I can either make this quick and fast, send you back to wherever it is you came from, or I can drag it out until you beg for death. Either way is good for me."

"You don't know what is going on yet, hunter? You have no idea what is happening to this realm, do you? There is a tear in what this world knows as reality, a literal tear. The way things used to be is no more. There is a war coming, a shift in this world that will change everything. Humanity is about to fall asleep."

"You fucking monsters with your grandiose way of talking! Just spit it out already. You things talk like you're in a movie and you're to keep the suspense up. Just say what the fuck you mean before I pluck out an eye."

"You're going to kill me anyway, hunter, so why should I? I'm not like the others you have killed and sent from this realm back to their waiting bodies. There is no body waiting for me back there, I'm whole here. So do as you will. You want to cause me pain, be my guest. You want me to suffer? I strive to suffer. Soon you will be the one on the bad end of a blade, so do what you will. Nothing will remain as it once was. The great change is coming; the Porter has been found and nothing you do will close it. Now, get to it."

I looked down at Hickner, not sure what to make of what he said, and in a way, didn't care either. One thing I had learnt over the years of dealing with these beings was, they tended to talk too much, speak in riddles and loved to try to cause confusion. Better to just be done with it and move on to the next job.

I slipped the blade under the creature's skin, the blackness retreating from the cut, the vibrant blue and yellow returned even brighter than before. Hickner cried out for a long time as I worked, skinning him, and making sure he didn't die until I wanted him to die. I flayed flesh from him, removing flaps and showing them to Hickner with a smile on my face as I did. I hummed a song to myself as I worked, not loving the job at hand but knowing it had to be done and made the best of it. I would take the creature apart, piece by piece, and then burn it to ash. Once that was done, the ashes would be separated into three jars and buried in my backyard. My yard contained holding spells that would make it so the demons and monsters could not reuse that form. What happened to the actual creatures once they were dispelled from Earth was not my concern, though I had been told and led to believe that they simply went back to their own world, or to another close by. As long as I don't see them again, it's fine by me.

When I was done with Hickner, the ashes in jars that were tucked away into my side bag, I called the principal and let him know the job was done. I warned him about the mess in the gym and the blood in the boy's change room. I also told the principal how to send the payment for the job. In this modern world I had to be adaptable, so I accepted cash, credit card and PayPal. Whichever payment type you preferred.

Epilogue

Hickner did not find himself barrelling though tunnels of strange lights back to the place he originated from. Nor did he fall into the darkness that so many atheists and nihilists on Earth are sure is the fate of those that depart this world. Instead, Hickner felt everything that occurred after the skinning and the burning. The flames that had touched his skin echoed long after they had turned him to ash. Hickner also felt himself being separated and put into different jars before Dillon buried them in the Earth and trapped it under horrible spells that echoed in the dirt.

Part of the destroyed creature wished that he had never been tempted to go through the port, that the life he was living had been better and seemed more promising. He wished he wasn't just some loner, pushing through a so-called life day in and day out, working for others that were able to enjoy so much more. Hickner had hated its life so much, the carbon-copies, pre-manufactured days, that he was an easy target for Rector and the plan that he was forming.

Hickner had come to Earth with a specific job, had been sent to scout the planet for any dangers, but had failed.

He had failed long before meeting with Dillon; losing sight of the objective when it had discovered the school and the treasure of sweaty underwear and socks just waiting to be eaten. It had been a fool to get distracted by such a salty addiction, but there was no way to resist them once you knew they were there. From the first time Hickner had tried one pair of underpants, the mission failed.

Hickner wondered, trapped in those jars, if Rector and the others would still go through with their plan after finding out what happened. If they got word that there was a hunter on Earth, and that Hickner had been dispatched so easily, would they still use the Porter to come through whole, or just continue the old way of travel? The old ways would make it impossible for their ultimate goal to be achieved, but at least they wouldn't end up trapped underground, unable to live, hoping that someone would come to save their disconnected body. The old ways of coming to Earth were dead in Rector's mind, something he told all his followers. To make Earth fall to its knees, they needed to be who they were and make humankind bow to them.

Hickner could only hope that if they did, they would come to where he was buried and allow him to join in the fun.